Rainbow Bridge

RITA RUMGAY

Jan-Carol
Publishing, Inc
"every story needs a book"

Rainbow Bridge
Rita Rumgay
Published November 2017
Little Creek Books
Imprint of Jan-Carol Publishing, Inc
All rights reserved
Copyright © 2017 by Rita Rumgay

ISBN: 978-1-945619-48-9
Library of Congress Control Number: 2017961446

You may contact the publisher:
Jan-Carol Publishing, Inc
PO Box 701
Johnson City, TN 37605
publisher@jancarolpublishing.com
jancarolpublishing.com

For Anita, I miss you.
You were the best of us.

Letter to the Reader

I've had a lot of drama and challenges in my life. After being repeatedly told by friends, "You should write a book", I have taken the plunge.

My main goal was to write the type of book that I enjoy reading. Perhaps you can relate. I wanted it to be one of those, *I can't put it down* books full of humor and drama. After you have read the last page, I hope you will feel like you made a new friend.

Everyone has a tale to tell. Thanks for letting me share this one. Even though, it came out of my head, it became very real to me. I cried for Gem, laughed with her, and reveled in her success.

Happy Reading,
Rita

Acknowledgments

Family members and friends for their critique and suggestions, thank you for reading and rereading my manuscript and for your honesty and encouragement.

Chapter One

Gem Wilson was alone again. Sometimes, the world seems so empty. Especially on quiet, still Sunday mornings. More so on this Sunday, because it was a rainy, dreary day—and one of Gem's only known living relatives, her grandmother, had just died. Ruby Mae had put up a good fight, but the stomach cancer had won. Still, 89 is a good, ripe old age. It's strange, using the word ripe for someone getting old. It sounds as if they were ready for picking. She could picture God reaching down and plucking Grandma, like a peach off a tree.

Should she get out of bed at all today? Should she go to church as usual? Her grandmother would say, "Yes, life is for the living. Get on with it."

What can you say about Ruby Mae Wilson? She was the best cook ever, and, she had a green thumb all the way up to her elbow. Being a devout Christian woman, she had touched many lives, just as the pastor said yesterday at the funeral service. I think she would have been pleased with the eulogy: not so much for the words of praise, but for the gusto in Pastor McClendon's delivery. His robust voice reached such a pitch of bringing God's presence down that the mourners forgot to cry and started exclaiming amen. It was agreed by all; she was sent off properly to her heavenly reward. The hardest part of it for Gem was leaving her in the cemetery. Knowing she wasn't really there, and yet her body was. At least she was lying next to Grandpa. They were together again. Gem could almost hear her mother's low, alto voice: "Groovy."

Being a product of a hippie parent has its drawbacks. Gem's mother wrote occasional letters from locations of different causes she supported around the globe, and had called on her birthday until the year she turned twelve. But Gem had not seen her mother since she was dropped off at Grandma Ruby Mae's, at the tender age of five. The letters stopped some years after that; the last one was from some place in Africa. Gem would sometimes mention to Grandma Ruby Mae that she wished she had been a cause for her mother to fight for, but Grandma would do that tut-tut thing with her tongue and say, "You are better off, child. You just don't know it yet."

As Gem grew older, she came to understand more about people from the hippie generation and the lifestyle that it entailed. She also learned through years of pestering her grandmother that something ugly and unmentionable had happened in one of the communes involving a druggie. It was so bad that it frightened her mother into finding a safe place for Gem to live. I suppose it was for the best. She was brought up in a loving environment, and her mother was free to rescue the world.

It was helpful to Grandma, too, since she was alone at the time, with no other relatives. She had lost Grandpa Henry to the war, which was always pronounced "wor in our world. Others called it "dubya-dubya-two." It was remembered as the one to end them all. But don't we tend to think the last big hurdle will be just that, the last one? Seems silly when you consider it; as long as there are politics and religion, there will be war. Sometimes I think men just need some—any—tiny excuse to fight or bully each other. I wonder if things would be any different if women were in charge; I know they wouldn't want their children killed, and everyone would be more conscious about their hygiene.

The last year had been rough, with the cancer slowly claiming Ruby Mae. She was determined to have the house in tip-top shape before passing on. It was an old farm house with an old-fashioned veranda around three-fourths of the first level. The second level had a landing at the top of the staircase with two bedrooms, a bath, attic storage, and a linen closet. The first level had a bedroom, formal dining room, bath, spacious kitchen, mud and laundry room, and the living area that was once called the parlor. The barn had been converted into a garage many years ago. Gem especially liked that the original rooster weather vane still sat at the top.

As for improvements, they replaced the weatherboard with new aluminum siding, put new shingles on the roof, and had the wiring and plumbing inspected, as well as the fireplace and flue. Gem's only worry now was how to keep it—or if she should try to keep it. They had emptied their savings to make the improvements on the house. The idea was to sell it so Grandma could go to assisted living, but she ran out of time.

A clap of thunder made Gem jump, and brought her thoughts back to the present. At least they had fixed the house up, and the roof wasn't going to leak for at least 20 years, according to the roofer's guarantee.

Suddenly, the power went out. That did it. She decided it was best to stay in today. The world could go on without her one more day. She was sure to find much to busy herself, what with the thank-you cards she needed to send for the food and flowers from the many friends and acquaintances of her grandma.

She padded barefoot into the homey country kitchen and lit a candle at the spacious table, surrounded by her grandma's ladder-back chairs. Scratch that; they were now *her* table and chairs. The room was silent, with the exception of the rain pounding on the new roof and the occasional clap of thunder. She felt safe, loved, and at home. *Now to those thank you notes*, she thought.

Gem had soon completed her task. There weren't many; most had made contributions to the church. Others gave to her grandmother's favorite charity, the Serenity Shelter for battered women. The church and shelter would send responses for those contributions. She put the readied envelopes in her mail out cubby on the roll-top desk next to the entryway, and made a mental note to drop them at the post office the next morning.

She washed up the dishes from her attempt at breakfast, if you could call a bowl of cereal at 3 a.m. breakfast. She did an inventory of what foods to freeze that were crowding the refrigerator. The tradition of bringing food to families when there was a death was alive and well. *It would be a shame to waste so much food.* She wouldn't be needing groceries for a month.

They had survived on Grandma Ruby's income from Social Security. Gem quit work and gave up her apartment to care for her grandma. She didn't enjoy that office job anyway; there was so much competition and backstabbing. She must be missing the gene of ambition, because she had never quite fit in there. The thought of going back to something like that filled her with dread. She would begin a job search tomorrow, maybe, if she could drag herself out of bed.

She recognized the signs. She had become depressed again, a familiar state for her. Trying not to think about that time, years ago, was like touching a sore spot in your mouth with your tongue: It's best to leave it be and let it heal. She should pull up her boot straps and carry on; only problem was she liked to wear sneakers, and didn't even know the meaning of that old saying. *Do they still make boots with pull up straps? Who knows?*

Just then, the power came back on. "Thank you, Lord," she said, her voice echoing through the empty, still house. There is nothing like losing something for a while to increase the appreciation level. Maybe she would get a pet. Grandma never allowed pets in the house. She found the thought of a soft, furry cat to welcome her home each day very comforting. Her life was going to change again. She hoped she was ready for it.

December 26, 1939
Merry Christmas Everyone.

Dear Diary,
My Ma gave me you to put down my thoughts. I guess it
may be on account of my moodiness as she calls it.

Pearl Harbor and the war has put us all in foul spirits.
I'm to write my thoughts as I have them. Not sure what
good will come of it, but I will aim to do my best. As I'm
putting these words down, bothersome things come to
mind.

I may hold off to another day to put them to paper.
That's all I know today.

Yours truly,
Ruby Mae

Chapter Two

Monday morning came, just as it usually does. Gem was surprised that she had slept so well. She had her coffee on the back porch. Her mind was flooded with the memory of Ruby Mae, and the first cup of coffee she was allowed to have. It was one of those cold, crisp fall mornings, in her senior year of high school. A real rite of passage moment, when Grandma handed her the steaming cup. Gem didn't even like the taste, but didn't say so. She didn't want to look foolish in front of her grandma, or disappoint her. That was long ago, another life. Now she enjoyed coffee very much, just like Ruby Mae had. The morning air was so clean and fresh; she stretched and filled her lungs. Feeling somehow renewed, she decided today would be a good day, a good day to start a new life. *Back to the salt mines for you, Girl.*

Gem sat down at the roll-top desk and opened up her laptop to polish up her résumé. She was amazed by what little experience she actually had in the working world. Of course, there was the associate's degree from Roane State Community College in business, but she had only actually worked at two jobs. One was a part-time position at a bakery; she had been employed there while in high school and during college. The other job was at Hopson Real Estate, where she had done her internship and stayed on as an administrative assistant.

Compiled, that equaled over twelve years of experience, but would that be enough? She had left on good terms and felt safe using them as references, along with Pastor McClendon, who had known her since childhood. It would have to be enough; there was no more she could do to make it more attractive. She hit the print button.

What is it about applying for a job that makes you question everything about yourself? How you look, how you talk, how smart you might be. . . Can I handle all this?

Remembering how unhappy she was at her last position, she decided to look at the want ads for something totally different. *Maybe something to do with health care would be good.* She had experience: taking care of her grandma during her illness. That should count for something.

She began a search for the Sunday paper. Most jobs were now found on the internet, but she wasn't much of a computer jockey and still liked the old-fashioned way of applying face to face. Sending an e-mail with personal information attached was a scary thing to do. She didn't like the idea of it floating around in cyberspace.

Pushing aside items on the sofa—used tissues, Grandma's photo album, and an old quilt, soft and thin from years of use—she located the newspaper. Scanning the paper's classifieds, she couldn't determine much from the small ads. Under miscellaneous, she noticed an ad for a landscaping company. It was the company's title, In the Garden, that caught her attention. It was also the title of a terrific old hymn that she had sung very often with her grandma as a child. Although it wasn't one of her favorites, like "How Great Thou Art," it still brought back warm memories. The rest of the ad gave information about the modest pay, with periodic raises and regular hours—*why not apply?* It would be different and she loved gardening. Ruby Mae had insisted on having a full garden every year. They sold most of it to the open-air market next to the highway, and canned or froze the rest. She felt her spirits begin to lift. Things were going to be okay; she could do this.

After she had tried on her third outfit, navy dress slacks and a collared white cotton blouse, she decided it would be sufficient for a first impression. Brushing her short dishwater blond hair, she then applied modest makeup. After all, it wasn't like she was going to the prom—*and just how made up do you need to be to appear suitable for working in the dirt?* Checking her reflection in the full-length mirror, she realized how much weight she had lost. She had needed to lose some, but she wasn't happy with the way her cheeks had that sunken look. Her blue eyes still had some sparkle, though. *Look out world, don't count me out yet.*

She grabbed the ad to check the address, and noticed the blinking red light on the phone. She had forgotten that she had turned it off after the funeral on Saturday; she probably had a million messages. Resigned, she took a seat at the roll-top desk and played them through. Lots of well-wishers had left their condolences. There was also one from Carolyn, her friend for life, as they called each other. That one she would return. Surprisingly, there was also one from her ex, as in husband, expressing his concern and condolences. That one she wouldn't return. She had not heard from Bobby Jones since they had lost a child in her second trimester, after one of his violent outbursts. He then ran back to his mommy in his grief. The next thing she knew, he was divorcing her and marrying Miss Becky Newman. She was the dimpled cheerleader type. He now had two children, and was probably working on making it a dozen. *So much for high school sweethearts.* She was better off. *What a mama's boy.* He was always an aggressive person, and had become increasingly violent toward the end. Gem wondered if he treated Becky the same as he had her. *That was then, and this is now,* she reminded herself. Grandma would say that you can't drive forward looking in the rearview mirror.

She decided to call Carolyn before trekking out into the big bad world. They had been friends since the third grade. Carolyn had relocated from Chicago to the small town of Clinton when her father got an engineering job at Oak Ridge National Laboratories. They had developed a friendship out of need and necessity. What with Gem being an illegitimate, abandoned child that the other children weren't to consort with, and Carolyn being the only black person in her grade that year, they gravitated toward each other. They were friends and defenders all through school, and had remained close. Clinton schools had been integrated since 1956, but some people still held on to a strange hate that

Gem could never understand. *Why couldn't they look past skin color and see how wonderful Carolyn was?*

Carolyn Woodward was as honest and straightforward as anyone could possibly be. She was educated, getting her master's degree in design arts, and refined. She had the kind of class that the royal family would applaud. Carolyn was also very successful, with her own design business. She and her husband George had married just after graduating from the University of Tennessee. He had a thriving business as an accountant. They had no children; Carolyn always joked that her business was her child, but Gem felt that she missed having children. It was probably why she mothered Gem so much.

Carolyn's clientele included people Gem would never even dream of meeting, such as public officials and sports figures. She would frequently fly all over the United States to perform magic for the elite's living spaces—not just rooms or homes, but living spaces. This notoriety didn't change who she was; she was still that down-to-earth and fun-loving friend that would shoot straight with her, even if Gem felt she didn't need to have a lecture.

Carolyn answered on the second ring: "Woodward Designs, Carolyn speaking." *She still answers her own phones, the personal touch.*

"Hello, Carolyn. I got your message, and thanks for the donation in Grandma's name. Your thank you note is practically in the mail."

"Okay, Gem, give it to me; what kind of morning are you having? Please tell me you aren't going to sit in the house and reminisce about old times. I could clearly see at the funeral that you are on the edge of a low. Let me help. You know, you could come to work with me—I could use a good right-hand girl." Her voice was kind and uplifting, but Gem knew she couldn't lean on her like a fallen over fence post. *I did that when Bobby Jones abandoned me. I have to stand on my own this time.*

"I'm doing well." Gem tried to sound upbeat, but her voice betrayed her with a little warble at the end. "Really, I'm great. I'm on my way out to find a j-o-b. Just wanted to return your message and touch base. Are you going to be in town this week? Maybe we can do dinner, or just hang out at the house." Gem could hear Carolyn's other line ringing; she was so in demand, Gem didn't see how Carolyn could have time for her.

"How's tomorrow night? I'll bring over one of those deli sandwiches you love so much, and we'll catch up."

She was bringing comfort food.

"No, please; I have enough food here to feed the population of New York City. Someone needs to help me eat it."

"Good luck on the job search. Remember, we're the ones who survived great obstacles, and we can accomplish anything we need to do. Whoever gets you will be lucky to have you. I'll see you tomorrow night, and I will bring my appetite." Gem could picture her bright smile.

"See you then—and thanks, Carolyn." Her kindness had made Gem tear up.

"You can thank me by getting back to your old self. I miss that crazy girl." She laughed.

"Bye." Gem laughed as well.

They both clicked off. *Leave it to her to take me from tears to laughter in just seconds.*

Carolyn always had a way of lightening Gem's mood and making her feel empowered. *Well, now I have something to look forward to, someone to eat with tomorrow night.*

I began to chant, "Job hunting we will go, job hunting we will go, hi-ho the merry-o, job hunting we will go," as I grabbed my purse, keys, and résumé before heading out the door. *Hold on to your hat, world; Gem Wilson is back. Well, maybe not back, entirely, but on her way.*

February 14, 1940

Oh Happy Day!

E.W. gave me a Valentine with hearts and flowers on it.
I'm not sure what to make of this. If he was to start courting me, H.W. would have himself a fit. E.W. tried to hold
my hand, sitting on the porch swing. I jumped up to get us
some refreshments. He sure thinks a lot of himself. I suppose a girl could do worse.

E.W. doesn't have 2 nickels to rub together. H.W.'s family
does have that grand farm. He'd never try to hold a girls
hand.

Just when I'm thinking my future is figured out, E.W.
has to go and give me second thoughts. Don't that beat
everything?

Yours truly,
R. M.

Chapter Three

I have a love-hate relationship with my VW, which I dubbed Ladybug. It saw me through high school and college without much trouble. But after that, we've more or less had a strained relationship with each other. She would go into the mechanic's shop a couple of times a year, and I would pay out lots of dough to get her back—until her next breakdown. But I couldn't bear to think of letting her go. I could drive my grandma's Crown Victoria, which I liked to call the pimpmobile. She acted as if she didn't like my calling her car that, but I would catch a small grin at the corner of her mouth when I said it. The car was as long as a city block, and drank gas like it was dying of thirst. But when Ladybug wouldn't start, it always would. Grandma's motto was: *If you take care of your things, they will take care of you.* Not that I had neglected Ladybug. She was practically a classic. It's a wonder she hasn't kicked the bucket by now.

Armed with my polished résumé, the classified ad, and my resolve, I set out to become one of the employed. Ladybug cranked over beautifully, just like she was raring to go, too. I made my way through the narrow, winding back roads to the highway and headed toward Clinton. In the Garden was located near the I-75 connection. This was prime real estate for a business. Its location made it accessible to several cities within a ten-mile radius.

As I pulled into the parking lot, the level of detailed organization was not lost on me. It seemed even the piles of mulch looked neat and tidy. Every stack of rocks, row of plants, and even group of greenhouses was uniform. I liked it already.

I chose a space that was shaded and backed the car into it, just in case I had to get a jump start. It was probably not going to be a problem, but this type of thinking has become a habit with the Ladybug and me. I put her in the park, yanked on the emergency brake, and cut the engine. As I made my way to the entrance, I said a silent prayer, requesting heavenly intervention on my behalf. I needed an income, and an outlet. If this place could provide both and be a decent place to work, that would be just what the doctor ordered.

There was a jingle as I opened the door, bells above the door saying, "Hello, someone's here." I surveyed the office surroundings. It didn't reflect the neatness of the product displays I had seen outside. There were stacks of books turned every direction on the floor, and precarious piles of paper covering the counter and the desk behind it. All I could think was *what chaos.*

Just then a lady who looked as if she were dressing for the prize of best 1970's librarian in a costume contest popped through a side door. Seriously, her hair was in a bun held up with a pencil. She was wearing some of those bigger-than-your-face glasses, a swirl-pattern blouse, a wrap-around skirt that hit just below the knee, and—brace yourself—Earth shoes. *No, my friends, disco is not dead.*

"Oh, hello," she said, smiling, with glossy pink lipstick. "May I help you?"

I must have been standing there with my mouth open. I finally found my voice. "Yes, I am here to apply for the position you advertised in Sunday's paper. I have my résumé and references." I pulled them out of my purse.

"Just have a seat," she said, motioning to a chair in the corner. I had not noticed it because it was covered with curtain rods and blinds. "Please excuse our mess." She shrugged. "We're reorganizing the office."

She cleared the chair for me, whipping up the items in it in one swift motion, and said, "Mr. Flowers will be right with you, Dear."

As I took the seat, I must have giggled at the irony of a landscape business owner being named Flowers, because she gave me a whimsical look over her shoulder as she hip-bumped her way into the door marked *Office*. "Someone is here to see you about the greenhouse job, Jack," she said.

I then heard a voice that sounded like it came from a tuba. "Send her in, Miss Polly."

Her name made me think of parrots and crackers, and I stifled another giggle.

"Yes, Sir," she replied. "You may go in," she said, motioning with her head because her arms were still full.

I stood up and approached the door. Miss Polly dumped her load of rods and blinds back onto the chair I had just occupied, and hurried out the same door she had entered. I was having *Wizard of Oz* flashbacks. What had I gotten myself into? Would they let me into the Emerald City?

I smoothed down my hair and straightened my blouse. Holding my papers in front of me, I entered the office. Sitting behind a desk that looked like it had been purchased at a yard sale—you know, the cheap kind, made of metal and obviously worse for the wear—was the largest, most red person I think I have ever met. Mr. Flowers overpowered the desk, the chair, even the room. His hair was so yellow, it looked like the sun. He had a complexion that was either a problem with high blood pressure, or sun exposure that was close to a first-degree burn. If he started changing colors like the Horse of a Different Color did in the movie, I was out of there.

There was nowhere to sit, so I stood there, being assessed by him as I was assessing him.

"So, you want to work for us?" he boomed. He wasn't in a foul mood: A person as large as he would have the voice to match.

"Hello, Mr. Flowers, my name is Gem Wilson. I am here to apply for the position you advertised in yesterday's paper." I tried to give a genuine smile, but it felt phony to me. I wished I could sit down. I offered my hand for him to shake.

"Oh, my!" he roared. "You must be Ruby Mae's grandchild." I was a little taken aback, and shocked at the reach of my grandmother's fame. He pumped my hand from his sitting position. It was a surprisingly gentle grip, for such a strong-looking man.

"Yes, Sir. I am," I nodded as I replied.

"Well, Miss Wilson, if you have even half the magic your grandmother had with plants and managing, I would be more than pleased to welcome you aboard." He motioned toward the window at the neat rows of product.

"Oh, I'm sorry. Please, may I offer my condolences? Ruby Mae will be sorrowfully missed." He bowed his head, looking genuinely sad.

"Yes, she will," I responded. "But she would want everyone to remember her in a happy way, and get on with life."

"You are so right!" he boomed again. One thing about Mr. Flowers, I didn't think I would have any trouble hearing him. "When can you start?" His eyes danced.

"Would now be good?" *If he only knew how badly I need an income.* Suddenly, I was feeling nervous. What exactly had I signed up for?

"You bet!" He laughed heartily.

I think I had my intervention. *Grandma strikes again.* She was something else. I really had no idea how influential she had been to this man. He was a stranger to me, but apparently not to my grandmother.

June 6, 1942

It's been a hard day today.

I'm in a quandary. E.W. has asked Pa for my hand. According to Pa, he's not in favor of it. His hat is set for me to marry H.W. because he has land and financial means

I'm not a girl given to spells of emotion, but H.W. doesn't make my heart beat against my chest like the attentions from E.W. Lord, help me, I've gone and fallen in love with a bad choice. What's a girl to do?

Tragically Yours,
Ruby Mae

Chapter Four

After my duties had been explained to me, I was happy to know that the disorganization of the office was Miss Polly's problem. My responsibilities were to assist in the management of the greenhouses. Mr. Flowers explained that it was the place where everything starts. "In order to keep up with demand," he said, "the greenhouses must produce what people will need down the road." In other words, I'd be working with the starting plants and would need to anticipate what would be popular for the next season. For the last few years, orchids had been the fad. I had seen them displayed in grocery stores, and in the garden department at local hardware and other stores.

Greenhouse planting was done with the same method my grandmother had used, only on a much larger scale. Saving dried seeds and growing your own starts not only made for strong, healthy plants, it also kept down the chance of infecting your garden with undesirable weeds, diseases, and pests from other growers.

My downfall will be in all the varieties of the plants. The names that my grandmother called them by will not be the same as a botanist would use. I hope my supervisor will understand. I may need to hit the library for that information. I will ask Mr. Flowers about that when the time comes. I don't want to ruin my chances of keeping this job.

As we left the mayhem of the office clutter, Mr. Flowers protectively held my arm and led me out the side door of the office. I was impressed with the walkways from one area to another. It seemed as if I was walking along a trail that could have been built in Ireland. The stone paths had three-foot-high walls that looked as if someone had put much love and care into them. Groups of trees with their balls of roots bound with burlap adorned each side. All were sorted according to type and size, with the tall ones giving periodic shade to the pathway. Various plants grew along the walls, creating a fairyland feeling.

Up ahead I saw a boy. He wasn't quite as tall as my 5'6". He had tangled curly black hair and coffee-colored skin. His clothes didn't quite match, and were hanging on him very loosely. As Mr. Flowers and I approached, I noticed he had many scars on his arms. He was dragging a hose behind him with great effort. He was also dragging his right leg. When he looked up and saw us coming, I noticed his eyes weren't quite focused in the same direction, but I could tell he was very happy to see us. He dropped the hose and opened his arms wide to greet us. Obviously, he had never heard of stranger danger, and he was making a direct path for me. "Hello, Pretty Lady," he said, beaming. He stood there with his arms outstretched, waiting for a hug.

I froze; I'm not sure I could say why. Maybe it was the dirt on his clothes, or because I was still feeling a little raw from my emotional weekend. I stuck my hand out to avoid the hug, hoping a handshake would do. Mr. Flowers put an arm around him and took the boy's arm with his other hand. He said, "Calvin, this is Miss Wilson." The arm hold had deterred the boy from giving me a hug. Calvin dropped his arms to his side and looked down, as if he was trying to figure something out. He then lifted a finger, pointing. "I say hello to you and shake your hand." His smile returned, and he looked like he had gotten a question correct on *Jeopardy*.

Mr. Flowers responded with, "Yes Calvin, very good."

I pumped his thin, dirty fingers and said, "Nice to meet you, and please call me Gem."

He said, "Nice to meet you, Gem. I work now." With that, he went back to pulling the tangled hose. I was already forgotten.

"That was very good, Calvin. I will come for you when you need to stop watering," Mr. Flowers called over his shoulder.

Mr. Flowers led me on down the path toward the greenhouses. "Calvin is a student in the Special Ed program at Clinton High School. He is part of a new transition program designed to integrate children with disabilities into a work environment, so they have some sort of function after graduation. He has been with us for about six months now. I couldn't ask for a better employee." He then shook his head. "I worry that he's neglected at home, what with his appearance. Foster care has its struggles, too." I couldn't help looking back. I had this haunted feeling, as if I knew Calvin from somewhere. I wondered what his life was like as Mr. Flowers continued to guide me toward my destiny.

When we rounded the corner, I saw a vision of complete loveliness. It was an oasis of palms, fountains, stone benches, and colorful plantings. Perfectly placed in the corners were a sundial, a bird bath, and potted Japanese maples. Overhead was a trellis that covered the entire area with climbing roses. There was just enough light to see the surroundings. So beautiful was the vision that it took my breath away. Water was coming out of stacked rocks and flowing over walls of porcelain tile. There were wooden benches placed next to clay pots full of ferns. *This must be what the Garden of Eden looked like.*

Mr. Flowers laughed, in his deep booming voice. "What do you think of our showroom?" He waggled his golden eyebrows up and down.

"Heavenly," I breathed out.

"It gets us a lot of interest. It's hard for a customer to *not* want something like this for their business or home," he said. "Ah, here we are; get ready to meet the man who is large and in charge," he said. We stepped through a wrought iron gate, leading to a cedar shake building marked *Greenhouse Management*. It was a large building, with a quaint entrance that had a small porch and chairs beside the door. On either side, there were rows of greenhouses; I counted eight altogether. As we stepped inside the management building, I saw rows upon rows of products obviously meant for maintaining the greenhouses. The smell of chemicals wasn't terribly pleasant, and burned my nose a little. To the right was a partitioned office with half walls about four feet high, and a row of employee lockers with name tags placed at the top. There was no one inside the building. Mr. Flowers pulled a walkie-talkie from his wide leather belt. "Evan, come in," he said, pushing the call button.

"Yes, Jack?" replied the mystery voice.

"Location?" responded Mr. Flowers.

"House Four," returned Evan.

"This way," said Mr. Flowers, pointing toward the greenhouses on the right of the small office building.

We made our way out of the management building, and passed three of the greenhouses. As we stepped into the greenhouse marked *Four*, I experienced sensory overload. The greenhouse had such an earthy aroma; it was almost like breathing pure oxygen. I pulled in a deep breath and felt somewhat giddy. This was going to be very different from office cubicles and the sound of ringing phones. And everyone seemed so kind here.

"Mr. Evan Walker, this is Gem Wilson, Ruby Mae's granddaughter. She will be your new assistant." Mr. Flowers motioned toward me.

I put out my hand to greet him, but he still had his back to me. He had on overalls, a white tee shirt, a black rubber apron, and work boots. Slightly balding, his remaining hair was a mousy brown-gray mix. "Doesn't make her the same as Ruby Mae," he said, without turning around.

I lowered my hand and looked at Mr. Flowers, waiting to see what I should do. "Don't take Mr. Walker too seriously; he's a bit of a grump."

With that, Mr. Walker spun around and said, "I may be a grump, but I am the best at what I do." His eyes were a piercing blue, and his face was stretched tight. You could tell exactly the shape of his skull. His lips were thin, and in a grimace showed smoke-stained teeth.

I took a step back, not sure how to respond to this Creature from the Black Lagoon type.

"Pay no attention to him," Mr. Flowers said very kindly. "He's a lot of wind, without much behind it. We couldn't run the place without him, and I think once you two get to know each other, you will click just fine." He winked at me.

With this, he left us to get acquainted— or more estranged, I'm not sure which.

September 30, 1942

Love is such a tender thing.

We met down by the creek for a picnic.

The sun was so warm. His smile, so sweet. I wanted to stay that way, forever.

I pray God will understand the things love does to your soul.

Prayerfully,
Ruby Mae

Chapter Five

After Mr. Walker handed me an apron, we spent the rest of the day together, but he said very little to me. He would give an order, such as, "Take these pots to number *two*," meaning greenhouse number two, and I would comply without comment. The rest of the day went on much the same, all the way until quitting time. He avoided looking directly at me. *When the time is right, I'd like to ask him just exactly what put the burr under his saddle.*

After being dismissed and told to be there promptly at 8:30 a.m. by Mr. Walker, I made my way back down the magical path. I was glad to be in the open air and by myself again. My clothes were filthy. *I'll need to dress more appropriately or bring a change of clothes tomorrow.* I couldn't help but pause and marvel again as I went through the area Mr. Flowers called his showroom. It would be a great spot for sitting and thinking. *Maybe I can have my lunch here tomorrow.* My stomach growled, reminding me I hadn't eaten very well today.

As I went through the office to make my way to the parking lot, I stood in amazement at the progress Miss Polly had made. Most of the room was in order. She popped up from behind the counter separating her desk from the rest of the room.

"Hello, Miss Wilson. If you wouldn't mind, please read over these papers and sign them where I indicated with an X. Then you will be an official employee. How did it go?" she asked, handing me the paperwork and a pen.

"All right, I guess. I'm not sure if Mr. Walker likes me or not. He seemed a little put off. Did he not want an assistant?"

"Oh, sure he did. He just has some things to deal with. I went back and warned him about you before Jack took you back. You see, he's my uncle. He has run things for Jack for a long time, but he's getting up in years and can't quite do the things he once did. Sometimes it's hard to admit our limitations," she said, wiping her forehead with a tissue and smoothing her hair back into place.

"I can understand that, but there seemed to be more to it than just resentment." I shrugged my tired shoulders. Looking over the W-2 and insurance forms, I signed and dated them, then handed them back to her.

"Well..." She took the papers looked toward the door. Then in a whisper, she said, "I probably shouldn't tell you this, but he was once in love with Ruby Mae, and you are the spitting image of her when she was your age. It was after your grandfather was declared dead from the war. Uncle Evan approached your grandmother with hat in hand, and asked to court her. I'm not sure exactly what happened, but she must have said no. He tried for a long time to get her to be his wife. Uncle Evan never married, never even tried to have a relationship after that. It seems no one could hold a candle to Ruby Mae." She shook her head sadly.

"Wow!" I was stunned. "That clears up a lot of things. Mr. Walker was right about one thing; I am not my grandmother. She was practically a saint. Just the fact that I'm related to her helped me get this job."

"Not just that, my dear. It was the last two years of care you gave her and your unselfishness that got you this job. Your sacrifice didn't go unnoticed. Not many would have done what you did, giving up their life to care for another." She looked at me tenderly. "You also have a great deal of gardening experience, which is rare these days."

I could feel myself blushing as I explained. "It wasn't really much of a life to give up, before I moved in to nurse my grandma. I was not happy. My marriage had failed, and my work was terribly unpleasant. I know you run this office, and Mr. Flowers seems like a very nice boss. Some offices have an atmosphere of pure poison. The politically correct term for the experience I had is a *hostile work environment*. I'm glad to be doing something different," I said, shifting my sore feet.

"Here's another bombshell for you. Mr. Flowers, Jack, is my husband. And yes, he is a good boss, but we aren't in that category. You see, we're partners. We both own the business." She laughed.

"Your husband? But he calls you Miss Polly." I was confused.

"It's just a pet name, and I like it. If you live long enough, you will eventually become Miss Gem to others. That seems to happen right at the menopause stage. If you can figure that one out, please explain it to me," she said wearily.

"If you have no more bombs to drop, I should be on my way home. I didn't exactly plan to be working right out of the shoot. I wasn't quite prepared," I explained, motioning toward my soiled clothes.

"You will be tomorrow. See you then." She smiled.

"Oh." I turned back toward her, "One more thing. Would it be out of line if I were to buy Calvin a decent pair of shoes?"

"Certainly not, but we've been down that road. It seems like whatever we buy him disappears." She shrugged.

"I see. Maybe we can think of a way around it." I waved goodbye.

She waved back.

I trudged to Ladybug on aching feet. My brilliant parking idea from that morning hadn't quite panned out. The day had become unseasonably hot for February, and the shade had shifted from my chosen parking space. I calculated which space would be in more lasting shade for tomorrow, making a mental note to park there instead. I cranked down the windows before sitting on the hot vinyl seats. I could feel sweat breaking out on my back. *What do you get when mixing dirt and water? You get mud.* I would not be walking into the house; I would be sliding in.

As I made my way from the highway back to the barely two-lane country road leading home, my mind drifted over the day. Everyone has a story to tell. I wanted to know more about Miss Polly and Mr. Flowers, as well as Mr. Walker. I hoped to have him like me at least a little. *And that* boy, Calvin, I wonder what happened to him? We are all just one accident or a few missing brain cells away from being like him. I hope someone is kind to him tonight. I need to get my thoughts on something else.* I could feel the tearing up about to happen.

"Please, God, protect Calvin tonight, and thank you for my job."

Before I knew it, I was pulling into the driveway. I stopped the car and left it idling. Walking around the back, I made my way to the mailbox. Bills and more bills were the contents. I would have an income soon, though, so it would all work out.

After pulling Ladybug into the garage, I stood looking at the house. I remembered only one other time when I'd felt this lonely. It was after losing my baby boy. The house was the same as I had left it, dark and still. *Maybe I should sell it and get a smaller place.* But I wouldn't sell yet; the experts say to wait a couple of years after someone's death before you make any big decisions. That was usually for spouses, though. I wondered if it counted the same for other losses too. I wondered if the experts on such things were people who had lost a loved one. My guess would be that most of them probably got their ideas from an education, instead of from personal experience.

I went through the house and turned on lights, the television, and the radio in the kitchen. I needed to fill the house with light and noise.

Remembering the power bill, I turned them off again, leaving only the radio on. It was tuned to the oldie station. They were playing "You Send Me."

What a day. I popped a plateful of leftovers into the microwave and headed for the bathtub. *I am sure to sleep well tonight.* It seemed every muscle ached. For some unknown reason, Calvin crossed my mind again: that big smile, and his innocence. *I wonder what he will be eating tonight? I hope no one is abusing him. Think good thoughts, Gem.*

Looking forward to the next day, I could hardly believe the one coming to an end. *I walked out of the house this morning looking for a job, and walked back in with one. Today has been a good day. My dinner with Carolyn is tomorrow night; I may have two good days in a row.*

It could happen.

November 4, 1942

Hard times are coming.

I have a great secret. I am so fearful. No one can ever know.
H.W. is joining up with the army. He wants to marry right
off. He's to leave by Sunday. I've a hard choice to make.

My heart cries for E.W. What a fix I'm in.

Ruby Mae

Chapter Six

My second day on the job proved to be less tiring than the first. The weather had turned into an early spring. A misty rain began before dawn, and continued all day. The landscape crews, not being able to work outside, were on hand to assist Mr. Walker and me. I was relieved not to be alone with him. The crews for In the Garden were mostly made up of Mexican immigrants. They all had very traditional Mexican names, like Juan and Carlos. I enjoyed listening to them speak Spanish to each other. I took Spanish in high school, but it didn't sound anything like theirs. They spoke so quickly that very few words were familiar to me.

Calvin was also working with us. Tilting his head back and feeling the rain on his face, he said God was doing his job of watering. It came out as, "God water for me today." He and I cleaned out the beds and tables in greenhouse two to prepare for the summer ferns and spring plantings. He was a very hard worker but moved slowly between tasks, dragging his leg. I couldn't help but notice that his teeth were badly in need of cleaning, and he was missing some buttons on his shirt. His shoes never seemed to be tied. I offered to tie them, but he just waved my hands away.

I complied, but it drove me crazy all day.

He stumbled over his broom and came out of his left shoe. I picked it up to hand it to him and peeked inside to check the size: eight.

On my way home, I made a detour to Walmart. I picked up a bag of socks and slip-on leather work boots for Calvin. It wasn't in my budget, but I had to do something.

After arriving home, I opened up the drapes in the living room. The rain had let up some, but it still looked gray outside. I planned out a meal of roasted chicken and steamed vegetables with yeast rolls; all I had to do was heat the already-prepared food. After my bath, I felt almost human again. I probably should have invested in some high-powered laundry detergent, or grabbed a couple of gallons of bleach while I was at the store. I could see designated sets of work clothes in my future.

After loading the washing machine, I put the dinner on to heat. Carolyn would probably arrive around 7:00. I settled into the sofa and switched on the news, just in time to see a sunny forecast for the next week. I must have dozed off; The next thing I knew, Carolyn was shaking me. "Wake up, Sleepyhead. Dinner is served."

I blinked and rubbed my eyes. "Oh, no! Is dinner ruined?" I asked as I jumped up.

"No, thankfully. I must have come in just as you dozed off, because it wasn't even warmed up yet," she said, looking at me with a worried expression.

"You look great, Carolyn. I'm so glad you're here." I felt myself slowly coming around.

"Let's eat and catch up with each other. I need to hear some of your glamorous stories, so that I can live vicariously through you," I said, pulling her toward the kitchen. I wanted to move the conversation away from me. I didn't feel like being mothered just then.

We lit candles in the dining room, then took our loaded plates and iced tea in there to eat. Carolyn filled me in on her last customer. She unbelievably wanted a waterfall, of all things, in her bathroom. The customer was a wife to a big-time country music star and was accustomed to getting what she wanted when she wanted it. It took some doing, but Carolyn had managed it by using specialty plumbing products, normally used for landscaping.

"You're a genius!" I exclaimed. "What did it look like? Was the customer satisfied?"

"Yes, it is a very nice, and pretty, miniature waterfall." Carolyn gestured the shape with her hands. "She settled right in. But guess what she wants next?" She raised her perfectly shaped eyebrows, making her brown eyes look even bigger.

"What, a rain forest in her kitchen?" I teased.

"No, she wants a revolving bed in her bedroom, so she doesn't have to turn over to see her TV. She could just turn the bed around for a better view—just a matter of convenience, you know. I have my doubts about that being the actual reason." Carolyn wiggled her perfectly arched brows up and down.

We laughed out loud in unison.

"I hope she doesn't get too dizzy," I joked.

We laughed until we were holding our sides, with tears in our eyes. Carolyn started spinning her forefinger in the air and wheezed, "'Round and 'round she goes." This made us laugh harder.

I gasped for air, eventually able to say, "It feels so good to laugh again."

Feeling somewhat recovered, I remembered that I wanted to share my day. "Guess what? I got a job yesterday."

She regained her composure and sat up with rapt attention. "Tell me all about it."

"It is like no other place I have ever worked." I sat sideways in my chair, facing her. "There are such characters there. The owners, Jack and Polly Flowers—yes, that's their real names—Jack is this huge, bright yellow-haired man with a voice to match his size. He looks like he just came in from a fishing trip, all red and windblown. His wife, Miss Polly, runs the office. She's like a disco queen-slash-librarian type from the 1970s, but she is so kind and motherly to all the employees." I leaned in closer to Carolyn. "The most perplexing and colorful of all is Mr. Evan Walker, Miss Polly's uncle, who had this huge thing for my grandmother. He would win if he were in a contest with Oscar the Grouch for who can be the most abrasive."

"Sounds like a cornucopia of personalities." She smiled. "Also sounds like you have found your niche, Gem girl. You always did well with gardening, and I know you despised that unruly mob scene at that office job."

Excited to tell her everything, I continued on. "The landscaping crews are mostly Hispanic and local high school kids that are saving for college through co-op programs. But there is one boy who is stuck in my brain. His name is Calvin, and he's a special needs teenager who is in foster care. He has a lot of scars on his arms, his clothes don't match, and his shoes are falling apart." I frowned. "I don't think he's getting the care he needs."

"Well, you could call children's services, if you think there is something to report," she said.

"I'm not sure yet. If I don't see any improvement, I may consider doing that."

"Tell me more about this guy who had a thing for Ruby Mae. He sounds like a man with a past. I find that very entertaining," she said, resting her chin on her palm with her elbow on the table.

"Well, it seems he was attracted to Grandma sometime after Grandpa Henry passed away, but she wouldn't have anything to do with him. When Mr. Flowers introduced us, he wouldn't even look at me. He tried to keep it up all day long, but I caught him making quick glances my way. When I was leaving for home, I asked Miss Polly about him not liking me. She said it was probably because he had run the business alone for many years, and is now in need of help. I think his pride may be hurt. And Miss Polly told me that I look so much like my grandmother did when she was my age, that it may be an unpleasant reminder of the heartbreak he experienced. I sure hope I can learn to get along with him, and establish my own identity. It is really hard to live in someone else's shadow," I shrugged. "Grandma Ruby Mae cast a very long one."

"How could anyone help but love you?" She slapped the table. "You're only the nicest person that ever existed."

"Oh, shut up!" I said jokingly.

It was like we were still in high school, talking about a mean teacher. Some people have a way of making you feel a childlike youth. That was just one of many of Carolyn's gifts.

November 9, 1942

Dear Friend,

I am tied to H.W. We wed in his folk's church on Saturday.
Our time of being intimate was brief and left me with no
comfort.

We honeymooned at the old homestead. It was as if I could
feel the ghosts that once lived there mocking me. He leaves
for the Army today.

Pa is happy to believe that I am settled and proper.
E.W. what must you be thinking of your apple blossom?

Ruby Mae,
the Deceiver

Chapter Seven

Gem was enjoying her work at In the Garden, with the exception of the cold shoulder from Mr. Evan "Never Going to Like You" Walker. She was also enjoying working with Calvin. She now understood why Mr. Flowers considered him his best employee. She had never seen anyone work harder, or with a better attitude.

However, when Gem had presented the new work boots to Calvin, he drew back as if he was afraid they might bite him. She was perplexed, but didn't try to force the issue. She placed the new shoes and socks in Calvin's locker, and told him they would be there whenever he wanted them. She couldn't help thinking that she still had a lot to learn about Calvin and his mental condition.

On Friday, she proudly took her first paycheck in two years to deposit at the bank, where she'd had an account since she was fifteen. Ladybug was so low on gas that she had driven her grandmother's Crown Victoria that morning. As she was making a left turn into the bank parking lot, she saw flashing patrol car lights in her rearview mirror.

What did I do? she wondered, panicking. *I'm sure I used the blinker. I have my seat belt on. I hope I put the registration in the glove box. Oh, man, this is all I need.* She checked her reflection in the rearview mirror and smoothed down the cowlick in her bangs. Her eyes were bloodshot. *The cop will either think I'm very tired and be merciful, or he'll give me a breathalyzer test.*

As the officer approached the driver's side of the car, Gem lowered the window slowly.

"What is the problem officer? Did I do something wrong?" she asked timidly.

"No, Ma'am, but your tags have expired. May I see your license and registration, please?" he said, removing his sunglasses.

Gem couldn't help noticing the strength of his forearms, or the long dark eyelashes that framed the most beautiful green eyes she had ever seen. She then realized she had been holding her breath, and let it out slowly to calm herself.

"Uh, just one moment," she said. Gem fumbled with her wallet and searched the glove box. Somehow, she managed to get the correct paperwork.

"I'm usually very responsible," she stammered. "This is my grandmother's car. She passed away recently, and I am not quite sure what to do with it just yet."

Thank goodness she had changed out of her work clothes and combed her hair before leaving work. She then felt angry at herself for worrying over her appearance.

"I'm sorry for your loss, Miss Wilson," he said reading her name from her driver's license. "But you must get the tags updated every year. It's the law."

That's when I saw it. He was staring at me as if he knew me, but couldn't quite place me. Slowly, a little smile formed around perfect teeth.

"Yes, I will, Officer Garrett," I said, glancing at the name tag on his uniform. *Man, he is too good looking.* I made a quick inspection of his left hand. *And guess what? No wedding band, or tan line where one was. How is this guy single?*

"Um," he said, clearing his throat, "you may pay this ticket at the courthouse. Be sure to bring proof of your tag purchase. If you wish to contest it, the court date to do so is listed on there. Please sign here." He indicated the place with his pen. As I took the pen from his hand, our fingers touched. It was electrical. I signed something that looked vaguely like my signature and handed the pen back, avoiding direct contact. He tore the ticket out of his booklet and handed it to me, along with my license and registration papers.

I almost fumbled the exchange. This made him smile again. I liked seeing his smile. Was he flirting with me?

I suddenly felt a moment of terror. *What if I never see him again? Will I go through life breaking the law with the hope of running into him, becoming a hardened criminal?*

"Well, be safe," he said holding his hand up in a goodbye gesture. He acted as if he wanted to say something else, but turned and put his sunglasses on, heading to his patrol car.

"Bye," I said, watching him in the rearview mirror.

Well, at least I have a male encounter to tell Carolyn about. I think Officer Garrett is the one that is breaking the law. It should be illegal to be that good looking. Oh, how am I going to be able to afford this ticket and buy tags? Well, so much for finally getting a paycheck. I need to get my head out of the clouds. I am acting like a teenager on a chocolate high or something.

Gem watched as the patrol car pulled back onto the highway. He didn't wave or look back. *Maybe I imagined it all.* Either way, Gem knew she needed to unload her grandmother's car, and fast. She decided to park it at the mailbox and put a sign on the windshield. *If I go online, I can find out the blue book value. I should be able to sell it at that price.* The only drawback was that being such a big car, it was a gas guzzler. *And gas just seems to keep going up and up.*

Arriving home, Gem saw a crowd had gathered at the road. She stopped just inside the driveway as her neighbor, Mr. Johnson, approached the car. He owned the farm that surrounded the house and property. Grandma Ruby Mae had sold off most of the land to him before she became ill. She knew she would no longer be farming, and had no male heirs with the potential of farming the land.

"I was cutting hay, Miss Wilson, and saw a strange man at your door. It looked as if he was trying to break in or something," he said, putting his thumbs in his overall bib like a rooster about to crow. "I laid on my tractor horn, and he took off. Of course, it brought everyone else out, too." He motioned toward the neighbors who lived across the road. This was one community that responded to horns and alarms. It happened rarely, and usually meant there was an emergency.

"Thank you, Mr. Johnson," Gem said wearily. "Do you think I should call the police?"

"We called them, but they just took a description and said they would send someone out," he said with a shrug.

"Well, I got to be getting back to the fields, but I will keep an eye out." He waved, then climbed over the barbed-wire fence and headed back to his waiting red Massey Ferguson.

"Thanks again," Gem called out. *I was probably drowned out by the sound of his tractor motor.*

Hearing the exchange, the neighbors went back across the road. The show was over, so they headed back to their lives.

Gem parked the car and walked to the mailbox, collected the mail, then drove slowly down the gravel driveway. She stopped the car in front of the house and got out to assess the damage.

It looked as if a tire tool or some type of metal object had been used on the heavy wooden door. What the burglar didn't know was that the door also had a large, solid deadbolt. He couldn't have possibly gotten in by way of the door, not without some much heavier equipment. *I wonder why he didn't just break a window. What could I possibly have that someone would want to steal?*

Just as she turned the key, a patrol car came down the driveway. For a moment, Gem's heart stopped. Could lightning strike twice? Would she have a second encounter with Mr. Gorgeous in the same day?

No, it wasn't Officer Garrett. The patrolman was a heavy-set fellow: Officer Kramer. He examined the door, said he had a good description, and would be on the lookout for him. He also gave Gem a card with emergency numbers and said to call if anything else occurred. He requested to have a look inside, just in case. Gem opened the door for him and waited anxiously until he had made his sweep through the house. Satisfied that all was clear, he reminded her to call if I saw anything suspicious. When asked for the description that Mr. Johnson had given him, he gave Gem a basic redneck image: green John Deere baseball cap, red flannel shirt, battered blue jeans, and work boots. *That could be any good old country boy in the state of Tennessee.*

Gem thanked him and walked with him back to the front steps.

As he pulled away, Gem suddenly felt very alone and unsafe. Her grandmother had kept a revolver hidden in her bedside table. *Maybe I should get it for protection.* Gem hurriedly put the car away, then checked all the locks in the garage and the house before scrambling upstairs. She stood by the door to her grandmother's room. She hadn't been in there since the funeral. Gem put her hand on the door knob, but couldn't will her hand to turn it. She remembered her baseball bat, from when she was on the church women's softball team. Looking in her room, she found it in the back of the closet, propped up in the corner.

Gem carried it around the rest of the night, and jumped at every sound. She double-checked all the door and window locks before deciding to sleep downstairs on the couch. *Maybe I should get a big dog with lots of sharp teeth.* She pictured an enormous dog ripping someone's throat open and shuddered.

Stretching out on the sofa, Gem dialed Carolyn's number. She told her friend about the encounter with the unbelievably handsome policeman. She was thrilled to hear Gem had met someone that interested her. She was very descriptive about how fabulous he looked, and how excited he made her feel. She made plans to get together with Carolyn for Sunday afternoon. Gem didn't tell her best friend about the alleged burglar, because she would insist that Gem stay with her and her husband George. She mentioned something else she wished to discuss on Sunday, but wouldn't say what it was. She said it could wait until then. *Knowing Carolyn, it's probably the type of news you have to sit down for, so you don't fall over in shock. She does everything big.*

"Who was that masked man?" Gem said aloud, quoting a line from *The Lone Ranger* before surrendering to the darkness behind her eyelids.

June 2, 1943

Miracles still happen. I became a Mother today. I have decided to name her Brenda Jane.

I am trying to keep hearth and home going. A bad drought is on us I fear for the crops. A good rain would be so welcome.

Henry has stopped answering my letters I pray he is safe but imagine the worst. Lord, help me. My little girl is awake and hungry. My but her lungs are healthy.

Yours,
RM

Chapter Eight

I sat through the service at the church on Sunday morning, but couldn't remember two words that the Pastor said. I found myself wondering what Officers Garrett's first name was, where he lived, if he liked sports, or was he a bookworm? Then my mind shifted, focusing on Calvin. I wondered if his foster family attended church. *I think he would especially enjoy the singing. He responds with such joy when music is played in the greenhouses.*

I was embarrassed to be daydreaming during worship services. It bordered on being rude, not listening when the pastor is speaking. *God knows how human we are since He made us. He would understand our being lost in thought sometimes. For me, it has been more than the norm lately.*

I really should get organized. I still need to go through all of my grandmother's things and get her car sold. I don't want to wait any longer. With her long illness, it feels like I have already had the time to consider what should be done. I'll talk it over with Carolyn and see what she thinks.

Coming back to reality, I realized that everyone else was standing; I jumped up and joined in singing the final hymn. We had our closing prayer, and the congregation turned to leave. I just stood there, enjoying hearing their voices: discussions of where to have lunch, plans for the week, and the weather. *I love this church. It's a simple church, white painted wood, topped with a steeple that has a cross pointing heavenward. From the* stained-glass windows, I remembered the Bible stories of my childhood. Each window depicted the life of Christ, from his birth to his crucifixion. I had difficulty looking at the one where He is on the cross; it made me feel sad, knowing what He suffered there. The last one, of his resurrection, was my favorite. It represented hope, and has such brilliant colors.

As I made my way down the aisle, several families asked me to join them in going out to eat, but I declined, explaining that I was having a visitor that afternoon and needed to get on home. I appreciated their invitations and did have time to squeeze in a meal, so I guess I lied. *Sorry, Lord, I didn't want to experience that fifth wheel feeling.* It wasn't that they didn't make me feel welcome. It was just a reality; I *was* a fifth wheel. There was no getting around it.

When I arrived home, all was as I had left it; nothing had moved, and no one had tried to break in, thank goodness. I hoped that was an isolated incident, and that whoever wanted in the house had changed his mind.

After closing up the front of the house, I had a sandwich and hot tea on the back porch. *I'm glad it's getting warm enough to sit outside again.* The trees bordering the field, which was now Mr. Johnson's, had leaf buds all over them. *Ah, spring returns at last. Sometimes it is harder to tell in the South if the seasons have completely changed yet. We seem to bounce into so many temperature and weather changes, all within a short period of time. If I count correctly, we have already had two false springs and one late winter freeze.* A person in this part of the south had to watch the Weather Channel religiously, just to know how to dress. Layers were always a good idea. Grandma liked to say, "You can always take something off if you don't need it, but if you need it and don't have it... Well, that's a problem."

I knew there would be pollen to deal with soon. It seemed to coat everything with a hazy yellow every spring, making things look dingy. *Then the rains come and wash it all away. There is a lot of wisdom in nature.* I marveled in the order of how it all works together.

I busied myself with basic chores of straightening and dusting, but I couldn't help watching the clock. Carolyn should be here soon; I wondered what important matter she wanted to discuss. Carolyn's discussions usually involved a big change. The last serious one was just before I had left my last job and given up my apartment. Carolyn had encouraged me to use the caretaking time with Grandmother's illness to reflect on my life and career. It had been the right choice. I could see that now. At the time, I was just hanging on; no husband, no baby, no real purpose, and no fulfillment. I wouldn't say that my grandmother's illness was a good thing, but I wouldn't trade the time of growing closer to her while we were fighting the cancer together. In the end, we had lost the war—but we won a lot of little battles. Our relationship had always been close, but strictly as grandmother and guardian to a granddaughter. The relationship between us during the illness had become one of two women with a common goal of survival: not just surviving the illness, but healing past hurts and building future hopes as well.

Carolyn rapped on the front door at 2 p.m. She looked fabulous in her tailored, pumpkin-colored suit. She also had her briefcase and sample books with her. I could see through the peephole that there was a small moving van outside, and two burly men in T-shirts with the same logo as the truck: *We Move U.*

As soon as I opened the door, she grabbed me and hugged me hard, almost lifting me off the floor. "Girl, get ready, because here I come. You're getting a redo, and not a minute too soon."

"Wait! No, I can't afford it, and I won't take charity, Carolyn. Have you met me? I thought we were going to have a discussion. You know, where people sit and talk about something *before* it happens."

"Oh, hush," she said, gently pushing me backward. "I can do this, and I will. You have no choice. I am taking your house hostage. I can't stand it another minute. Don't get me wrong, I loved Ruby Mae like my own grandma, but she was so..." She shook her head trying to come up with an inoffensive adjective that described my grandmother's down-home style of decoration. "Frontier or pioneer, early Americana. There, I said it. And I am not ashamed, may she forgive me." She raised her opened hand to the ceiling.

I was stumped. Gazing around the room, with the rocking chair, the flower-patterned overstuffed sofa, and Chantilly lace curtains, I had to agree. The room was a time warp to the Forties, and it was shabby. We had paid close attention to the condition of the exterior and inner workings, upgrading the house, but not a dime was spent on decorating. "You're right. If I am going to stay here, which is a big 'if,' it would be nice to have it at least look presentable. But I insist on paying something. There has got to be some way I can be helpful to you."

I thought back on the night we had dinner and her story of the lady and the waterfall. She had used landscaping materials for that job.

"I know. I have an idea; why didn't I think of it before? You sometimes need plants and other landscaping products for decorating. And ta-da," I motioned with my hands open. "I work at a landscaping business. Maybe my connections at work could be useful to you. Would that be something you could use?"

"You know, that is a great idea," she nodded. "Do we have an agreement? Will you let me and my strapping friends outside get busy?"

I suspected that Carolyn would probably agree to anything at that point, just to get her way.

All I could do was nod, amazed at how blessed I was to have a friend like Carolyn. She was already motioning the men inside, pointing to the sofa and making an 'out of here' motion with her hand.

Carolyn's expression became serious. "Okay, now tell me about the break-in. And then tell me why you didn't say anything about it. You know this is a small community, and everyone knows your business. Don't bother giving me a brave speech, or pretending it was no big deal. I happen to know that Mrs. Johnson's gossip is very reliable." She folded her arms and cocked her sleek head to one side. "I bumped into her at the grocery store. She asked how you were, and if anything else had happened. Imagine my embarrassment at not knowing, and my concern for your safety." She narrowed her eyes at me.

"It wasn't a break-in. Someone left a few marks on the front door, trying to get it open. Nothing else has happened. Really, I'm fine. There is nothing to get upset about. It was nothing." I folded my arms, too. "It was just one of those things. Besides, what could I possibly have among all these old, dusty relics that anyone would want?"

"You never know. It could be a coincidence. Here you are alone. Unless your mother is still out there somewhere, your relatives are all gone now. There could have been a family secret, or some unknown treasure hidden somewhere, like under the floor or in the walls." She opened her arms wide and looked around.

"Really, Carolyn. Ruby Mae was not wealthy, and she lived a very chaste life. The possibility of any secrets or hidden treasure is...not very likely. You have such an imagination." It was my turn to shake my head at her.

"Just the same, I'll be on the lookout for anything out of the ordinary, and I would give some consideration to getting some protection, like a gun or a big ole dog!" Carolyn the mother hen was used to having the last word on things.

October 25, 1944

Thankful for the ending of another season. We survived another harvest. Still recovering from poor yield of 43 but me and my baby doll will have a roof over our head this winter. All of my letters to Henry have returned, unopened. He could be gone or he has had a change of heart.

I'll just keep putting one foot in front of the other til I know different.

Waiting and Wondering,
Ruby Mae

Chapter Nine

We spent most of the day tagging what antiques I wanted to keep and instructing the burly muscle men what to carry out to the moving van. We then had them arrange what was left in a place that would work well with our list of new items that I would need. We covered the remaining furniture with sheets, and assessed the flooring.

Fortunately, the bathrooms, one upstairs and one downstairs, met with Carolyn's approval. We only needed new curtains and linens for those. The kitchen actually wasn't bad, with the exception of the floor having worn path marks. Carolyn suggested pulling up the linoleum and replacing it with ceramic tile. She wanted to replace the appliances, but I put my foot down. The stove was fine. "Just because something is old doesn't mean it isn't useful," I said. Besides, I knew this stove. I never had to guess if the temperature was going to be right. It was reliable and predictable. I didn't want to break in a new one.

The other rooms just needed a new coat of paint and curtains. It wasn't as dismal as I had expected. The one room we had left to deal with at that point was my grandmother's. I was glad not to have this task to do on my own.

Carolyn bravely opened the door and marched straight in. I hung back a little, hesitant to breathe in all the smells that would inevitably bring back memories of sickness and heartache. She turned to me and instantly understood my reluctance. "It's okay," she said, comforting me. "If it gets too tough, we'll come back later on."

There sat the hospital bed. Carolyn put a sticker on it that would tell the movers to take it out to the van. I was glad she was there to do that; I didn't think I could touch it. "Grab some of those boxes in the hallway," she instructed me. "We'll fill them with her personal items, and you can go through them later, when you are ready." I nodded and complied.

We opened the dresser that contained Ruby Mae's clothing, mostly under-garments and nightgowns. She never wore pants; her homemade dresses hung in the closet, winter sleeves on the left and summer on the right. To Grandma Ruby Mae, an orderly life meant an orderly mind.

After we had filled a box with the contents of the first two of four drawers, I made a discovery. The third drawer was completely empty, and the bottom drawer contained nothing but letters and envelopes full of photographs. Most of the photographs were of her family, and my mother as a child. The letters were tied with a red ribbon. All of them had foreign stamps, and military return addresses. Those were from my grandfather. Some were addressed to him and unopened. I supposed those were written after his death. Carolyn commented that the stamps would probably be worth something, if I wished to sell them to a collector. I shook my head, sadly. That's when I saw it: a floppy brown diary. My grandmother had kept a diary. *How interesting that I'll have her thoughts to read over*, I thought. I found great comfort in knowing that there was a recording of her life.

"Look!" I squealed. The cover read *Private Thoughts*. I couldn't open it fast enough, disregarding the word *private*.

It opened to a dog-eared page in the front. "Pa insists that I marry well. H.W. is his choice. E.W. has my heart. How do I go against my Pa? H.W. is making plans to join up for the war, making my decision dire. What's a girl to do?"

I flipped through some more pages. There were notes about the weather, her garden, and family illnesses. Carolyn was leaning so close to me that I could feel her breathing. "What does the last page say?" she asked, excitedly.

I turned to the last page. It only had two words written there: "He's gone."

"She must mean my grandfather. She must have stopped writing in the diary when she heard he had been killed. She must have been very sad to have written just those two words." I looked at Carolyn.

"That would explain the H.W., for Henry Wilson. But who is E.W.?" she wondered.

"I know! Evan Walker. That *has* to be it. E.W. Evan Walker, wow. Ruby Mae was a player." With the image of my S.A.S. Bass-wearing, white-haired grandmother having two beaus on the hook, we both laughed in spite of ourselves.

"No wonder Mr. Walker hates me. He wanted to be her husband, and she chose to marry someone else. Not because she loved him more, but because she didn't want to go against her father. Miss Polly got it wrong; she thought her uncle was pursuing my grandmother after my grandfather's death. I wonder what else we don't know. People really kept secrets back then. It sure was a different time. These days, when someone marries for something other than love, it's usually for money, but certainly not for sacrifice." I wasn't sure how to feel about that. The word *martyr* came to mind.

"Do you think she was happy?" Carolyn asked.

"I think she chose to be happy no matter what her circumstances, just like Paul in the Bible. Even when he was in prison, he praised God and told others what wonderful things God had done for him."

"Let's box up all these personal things and start on the closet." Carolyn was changing the subject.

"Why do you do that?"

"What?" she asked, with pretended sincerity.

"Whenever I mention religion, God, or the Bible, you squirm like a worm on a hot brick."

"I have issues; you know that I've always had issues in that department. Please, let's finish in here. I promise we can discuss it another time," she stated flatly.

"Okay." I decided I would let it go—for now. Something must have happened to make her turn away from religion. Several other subjects were also off limits, for the health of our friendship. Like politics: She was a Democrat, and I leaned toward Republican because of the right-to-life situation. We also didn't discuss race. I had no way of knowing what it was to be black, and didn't think of her as a black person. She was just Carolyn, my best friend, and a strong, intelligent, successful person. But I knew she had been treated badly in school. I was an eyewitness to her being called the ugly n-word, and without skipping a beat, they called me a bastard. We both responded with: "That all you got, you bunch of hayseed rednecks?" I was glad when they lost interest.

I took the diary and my grandmother's letters to my bedroom and hid them safely in the nightstand. I didn't want to read them just now, but I was glad to know I would have them when I was ready to wade through all that emotion.

Before Carolyn left, she made arrangements for the flooring in the kitchen to be done during the week, and for the painters to come and do the entire interior. We picked curtain materials and a color theme for each room from her sample books. She told me she would come by In the Garden on Wednesday, to discuss a contractual agreement for their products to be used in her business.

"I cannot believe how quickly you work," I said to Carolyn. "You are so good at what you do."

"Come home with me." It was an order, not a request. She wanted me home with her, where I would be safe.

"No, I'd like to tackle those kitchen cabinets. They need to be emptied and boxed up." That was my excuse, and I would not be persuaded to abandon ship.

"I can see by the set of your jaw that there will be no compromise," she said, placing her hands on her hips. "If you hear any unusual noise, even if it's a mouse passing gas, George and I will come running."

"Thank you, for everything. I don't think I could have done any of this without your help. You have been an answered prayer. Oops." I covered my mouth with my hand.

"I pray too," she insisted, "just not out loud, and not for every little thing. I will send one up for you tonight. I don't like leaving you here alone. I meant what I said; call me, even if you just feel afraid." I nodded in agreement and saluted her.

With a "Toodles!" over her shoulder and her head held high, she left with the muscle men and their van crammed full of my old life.

December 24, 1944

This is a sad day. The telegram came today. It was just
as I had feared, I am a widow. I've a funeral to plan.
Grief is stuck in my throat. I can hardly speak or eat.
Dear Lord, is this punishment for my deceit?

Brenda with her full little face and chubby hands will
never know her Pa.

Heavy Hearted
Mrs Henry Wilson

Chapter Ten

Ibacked Ladybug into her spot in the parking lot. It was an overcast, dreary Monday morning. I seemed to ache all over. I think I overdid it with all the boxes I lifted and carried the day before. I also stayed up too late. After I had finished cleaning out the kitchen cabinets, I read my grandmother's diary from cover to cover. There were several pages in which she hailed the work ethic and family loyalty of Evan Walker. She had also mentioned how she liked the color of his eyes. I wondered why she didn't make a life with him after my grandfather passed away. Was it because she had my mother to bring up? I had no way of knowing. I wished the diary had continued. There were also some pages missing; they had been torn out. Maybe, if Mr. Walker could get past his anger, he could fill in the blanks. I stuck the diary in with my clean clothes to take to work. It was like having a bit of Ruby Mae with me.

I didn't have much thinking time the rest of the day. Miss Polly, looking sparkling in her tangerine pants suit with a gold lamé collar and matching headband, ran out to the greenhouse office with several orders. I seized the opportunity and scheduled a time for her and Mr. Flowers to meet with Carolyn on Wednesday. Miss Polly, who knew of Carolyn's reputation with Woodward Designs, was thrilled to have the chance to conduct business with her.

Calvin and I were so busy the whole morning that we almost missed lunchtime. He reminded me with a growling stomach that he hadn't eaten. He sometimes didn't have any lunch with him, so I had packed an extra sandwich and drink for him, just in case. I thought again that I would like to meet his foster family to talk about how to make things better for him, and get some answers concerning his care. He and I ate lunch in our Little Eden, the name I gave to Mr. Flower's so-called showroom area. The small fountain pond had been stocked with koi, and birds were nesting in the trellis above. It was like a Disney movie; it seemed like the seven dwarfs and Snow White could happen by at any time. Calvin only ate part of his sandwich, feeding the rest to the fish and the birds. *Note to self: bring more bread tomorrow.*

I hadn't seen Mr. Walker all morning. He was busy making arrangements for the crews to start the landscaping for a new subdivision going up in Oak Ridge. The city had demolished some of the row housing that had been used as living quarters for the Manhattan Project during the Thirties and Forties. Progress marches on.

Mr. Walker came around the corner, headed for the wrought-iron gate that led to his office.

"Mornin'," he said.

"Hi, to you, Mr. W.," Calvin answered with his sideways grin.

"Morning, Sir," I responded, hoping the respectful greeting would be noticed.

It wasn't. His steps didn't even slow down.

After lunch, Calvin and I had completed most of the orders. The high school boys and girls, working on their agricultural co-op for class credit, had loaded them for delivery.

I was—and at times, I am still—amazed by the intricate, organized ballet of Mr. and Mrs. Flower's landscaping business.

The only hiccup seemed to be with Mr. Walker, still. *I think it's time for a showdown. I've haven't done anything against the man. This cold shoulder treatment is getting old.*

I gave myself five minutes of being still during my afternoon break. If God could guide me, I was going to do my best to hear him. My mind kept coming back to the diary. *It should go to Mr. Walker. I have her letters and so much more. It would be selfish to keep it, too.* He should know how my grandmother really felt about him. Maybe it would bring some healing. Let's face it; it couldn't make him dislike me more.

That wasn't possible.

As I stepped into the greenhouse office, I gave myself a couple of seconds to adjust to the chemical smell of pesticides and fertilizers. Mr. Walker was seated at his desk. I took a deep breath and made a straight line for him.

"Mr. Walker, I have some things to say to you. I am not Ruby Mae Wilson. Never have been, never will be. I cannot help resembling her in appearance. I hope that someday you can see past whatever this grudge is that you have against me, and get to know me for who I am." I held my shoulders a little higher and continued, "She was a great lady, and I will always respect and love her. I had nothing to do with decisions she made, or the life she led, before I came to live with her. Please stop being angry with me and accept me—or at the very least, treat me decently." *There, I said it.*

"Fine", he said, and went back to his work.

That one word was all he had to say after my speech.

"I have something for you." I held out the diary with my arm extended. He would either take it or refuse it. My face was becoming hot and my arm was growing tired, but I was determined to wait him out.

He timidly took the book. He read her name and suddenly looked very old and worn. I began to wonder if I had made a mistake.

"Thank you," he said, not quite to me, just to the air.

"You are more than welcome," I said very softly. It was like a shaft of sunlight was slowly breaking through the clouds. His blue eyes were becoming watery. I mumbled, "Well, back to work." I didn't want to embarrass him by seeing his emotions.

When I went in to change at the end of the day, he wasn't in his office. I thought I heard someone crying in the men's room, but I couldn't swear to it.

Maybe all he needed was to know that he had been loved. Every living thing needs that.

Mr. Flowers suddenly burst through the door. "Is everyone all right back here? Where is Uncle Evan?"

I nodded that all was okay, and pointed to the men's room. "What happened?"

"We had a robbery in the front office. Some Arab-looking guy came in, demanding we fill an order for a list of chemicals. Miss Polly panicked and called the police with her cellphone; she had it in her pocket. The guy became angry and impatient. He grabbed some cash from the register and bolted out the door. Go to the rest of the greenhouses and tell everyone to meet in the front office in five minutes." He put his hands to his head to calm himself. "Oh, Gem, stick like glue to Calvin. This could really set him off."

He then disappeared into the men's room. I didn't want to think about what condition he would find Mr. Walker in. I made my way to the greenhouses, hoping to find Calvin; fortunately, the handicap bus from school had already arrived to take him home, at the usual scheduled time. As I made my way from the number one greenhouse to number eight, I repeated, "Front office, five minutes, emergency meeting." I got a lot of questions regarding what and why, but I ignored them and repeated myself, adding, "Go, now."

After everything seemed secure, Mr. Flowers repeated what he had told me about the intruder to all of the employees. He then suggested we be extra cautious, and on the lookout for anything suspicious. When the Clinton Police Department arrived, I was mortified to still be in my work clothes. Mr. "Too Handsome for Words," Officer Garrett, was questioning each employee. I was equally dreading and anticipating my turn. I didn't know if I would faint or flee.

I didn't have any more time to consider my options. When it came my turn, Mr. Walker stepped in to speak for me, like he was defending a helpless child.

"She didn't see anything," he said. "No need to bother her with this." His face was stretched tight, and his blue eyes were blazing. Then he did the most unexpected thing: He put his arm around me. "She is my assistant, and works in the back of the property with me."

It was suddenly as if I were his pride and joy. I was speechless. Between

Officer Garrett's inquisitive green eyes and Mr. Walker's sudden turn, I couldn't even get my eyes to blink. I was dumbfounded.

Everything that happened after that was a fuzzy memory for me. Officer Garrett was smiling at me, with those perfect teeth dazzling. I wanted to say something clever, but couldn't seem to come up with anything. I couldn't even tell if he recognized me. With my unkempt appearance, that may not have been a bad thing.

People moved around slowly, talking to the other employees. They soon began to leave, one by one. The office cleared and the police completed evidence collection. I watched as the investigative officers began to go also, still in a daze. It was like I was under water. I barely remember floating to my car to go home. *What is wrong with me? Someone wake me up!*

September 4, 1948

I can hardly stop crying. Sent my girl off on a school bus this morning. This place never seemed so empty. Even with a dozen field hands, I feel alone.

Watch over my baby doll Lord and bring her safe to home.

Her loving mother,
Ruby Mae

Chapter Eleven

When I arrived home from work, I was amazed by the flurry of activity. Carolyn had the painters so motivated that the top floor was already completed. A new chintz sofa and chair had arrived, and was grouped with my grandmother's antique tables around the fireplace. I heard a saw humming away on the back porch. Apparently, the flooring men were already cutting the ceramic tile for the kitchen. Two Hispanic ladies greeted me with "Hola," and smiled from ear to ear like they knew a special secret. They were folding drapery that matched the sofa and chair. For the first time in my life, I was going to be color-coordinated.

I went through the house searching for Carolyn, and discovered all the finished products from the samples we had chosen were going into place— but no Carolyn. Bounding up the stairs, I poked my head into my grandmother's room. It was painted a soft yellow, with antique white molding. It looked bright, cheerful and inviting. A rose-colored comforter with gold piping adorned a cherry four-poster bed, stationed against the same wall as the entry door. I would have never thought to put a bed on that wall. That is why I am not a decorator. A framed picture of my grandparents on their wedding day sat on the matching night stand. Draperies the same color of the comforter hung at the window, pulled to the sides with golden tasseled tie-backs. It didn't look like the same room.

Down the hall, my old room had also been converted, with pale green painted walls trimmed in the same antique white. Light oak bookshelves that matched my twin bed lined one wall. An oak desk adorned with a new computer sat in front of a beautiful new bay window. I didn't remember ordering that window, or anything else in this room. Bermuda shades created a soft glow with the afternoon sun shining through the window.

As I passed the upstairs bathroom, I saw the new shower curtain and towels. The room was done in a combination of the colors used in the two bedrooms. The walls were painted a soft white with an eggshell finish. She had accented with gold and green towels. The shower and window curtains had all three colors in a paisley pattern of rose, green, and gold. The cup, soap dish, and toothbrush holder were all in the same pale green. The mirror frame, curtain rods, and towel racks were golden yellow. It shouldn't have all worked together—but there it was, in perfect harmony. I began to suspect that Carolyn was part magician.

I started to clomp back down the stairs and noticed the gleam of the handrail. It must have been sanded bare and re-varnished; all the nicks and scratches were gone, and it shone like a copper penny. Carolyn had framed some of the pictures we found in the bottom drawer of my grandmother's old dresser, and hung them on the wall above the staircase. The frames were made of the same gleaming wood as the banister.

The kitchen was completely dismantled. The cabinets, table and chairs, and appliances were all on the back porch. The new flooring was more than halfway completed, but would need to set for twenty-four hours before any traffic was allowed. Then it would need to be grouted. This was told to me by the threesome of t-shirt wearers that were on their knees, laying the floor. I asked them if they had seen Carolyn, but they didn't know for sure where she might be.

The painters in their white coveralls were setting up to get started on the downstairs. It would all be done in a uniform antique white, with the exception of the bath, master bedroom, and kitchen. Carolyn had said that she wanted to surprise me with that outcome. A vision of random waterfalls everywhere—or a revolving bed—crossed my fearful mind.

Suddenly, I felt I was in the way. I didn't have a clue as to how to help, or even if I should help. Everything seemed to be getting done so well without me.

Carolyn came charging into the living room, talking over her shoulder to her assistant, Greta. "Please let me know if that color doesn't match the swatch, Greta. You know paint always dries darker than expected." Greta confirmed her orders, then turned and scurried from the room, a woman on a mission.

"Welcome home," Carolyn greeted me with a hug, wearing coveralls. "What do you think? Be brutally honest." She was holding her breath.

"I think you are amazing. Not to complain, but...some of these things—which are very, very, beautiful—we didn't discuss. It was just going to be some paint, new curtains, and a kitchen floor. This is...beyond my financial capabilities," I explained cautiously, so I wouldn't hurt her feelings.

"Really, Gem." She patted my shoulder. "It wasn't a stretch for me; most of the supplies were things I had on hand. Other items were from favors I called in. It was no sweat. Just a few phone calls, and *poof*, everything we needed came together."

"How did you accomplish so much so fast? All these workers had to cost a fortune," I said in a low tone, so as to not be overheard.

"Oh, Girl, I scheduled them for this gig months ago," she waved her hands in the air. "When I saw you and Ruby Mae fixing up the house, I cooked up my own plan to do the inside. That's what I do, you know." She nodded her head confidently.

"I love, love, *love* it. It is like you looked inside my head and picked out everything that I liked." I wanted to say that God had blessed her with a gift and she was using it to minister to me, but I knew that might upset her. I just smiled and said a gracious "Thank you, so much!"

She beamed.

Later that afternoon, pizza was delivered. We all gathered on the back porch. It was strange to be seated at the kitchen table and be outside. I asked if they minded if I said grace. All nodded okay, even Carolyn. I gave thanks for the food and all the efforts of the workers. We ate our fill and all got to know each other better. Most of the crew members had worked with Carolyn for many years, with the exception of the cute little Hispanic women who were hired recently. They were new immigrants looking forward to becoming citizens, and were so happy to be in America; their dark eyes sparkled with joy.

I told everyone the events of the day. They all seemed to think that the man who demanded chemicals from In the Garden could be connected to a rumor about a terrorist movement reported on the national news. Apparently, there was a research project going on in Oak Ridge Laboratories. It had something to do with a supercomputer, all very hush-hush. If the project were to fall into the wrong hands, it could make them very powerful. *All the unrest in the world is terribly unsettling. Can't we all just get along?*

After much discussion about terrorism and crime, the crew returned to the jobs at hand. They worked until ten o'clock that night. The kitchen floor was laid and the painting was completed; they would return tomorrow to put everything in place. When the last of the crews had finished, they left for home exhausted, but enthusiastic about returning the next day.

Carolyn hung back to double-check everything. I could tell that she also wanted to get me alone, to question me further about what happened at work today.

I retold the entire scene, adding the unexpected response of Mr. Walker and the doubts I had as to whether or not my mysterious police officer, Mr. Garrett, had recognized me.

"He *cried?*" she asked, speaking of Mr. Walker's response to the diary.

"It had to be him, sobbing in the men's room," I responded.

"Wow. And he put his arm around you. It must have been either true love for Ruby Mae, or some strange obsession." She was lost in thought for a moment. "I think there was more to all this than just a thing for Ruby Mae. It deserves some investigation."

I knew what that meant; Carolyn had to know. She would dig until all was revealed. I was too tired to think any more about it.

"Stick a fork in me, I'm done," I said wearily.

"See you tomorrow. Keep the upstairs windows cracked for ventilation," she said, somewhat distracted. Before she headed out the door to her waiting BMW, she turned back to me and said, "About that policeman—if you are interested, you need to think of a way to show him. Otherwise, if you're both this pathetic at approaching each other, nothing will ever happen. Goodnight, Cinderella." She waved behind her back, not giving me an opportunity to argue.

I secured the windows and doors downstairs and dragged myself upstairs to settle in my old room for the night. It felt like I was in someone else's house. I had to dig through some boxes to find something to sleep in, and my toiletries. *What a day.* The last thing I remember thinking before surrendering to sleep was how much kindness I'd seen in Officer Garrett's mysterious green eyes.

June 6, 1956

Brenda, who now asked to be known as B.J. has graduated eighth grade today and is to start high school this fall. She uses words like neato and swell. I'm perplexed when trying to have a talk with her. She doesn't care for my company these days

We disagree on most things. The only things we seem to have in common is our last name and where we live. I figure not having a Pa has a lot to do with her surly nature.

Betty Johnson seems to think it's being a teenager. I've studied and studied on it and can't recall behaving that way or hardly being a young person. Back then, I guess we grew up quicker because times were hard.

Lord, give me the strength.
Ruby Mae

Chapter Twelve

I woke to a banging sound and sat straight up. After adjusting to the surroundings of my new room, I remembered the workers downstairs.

For anyone who has ever done remodeling or built a house, I salute you. The chaos alone would drive any normal person to the brink. Not to mention the loss of privacy and financial stress.

I grabbed my clothes and hurried to the bathroom down the hall, hoping to avoid seeing anyone before I was presentable.

I bumped into Greta, Carolyn's assistant, before I could make the corner. "Whoa, excuse me," she said politely. "We didn't know you were still sleeping. I will give you a few moments." With that, she turned and went back downstairs. Thank goodness it was her and not one of the men. I had slept in a t-shirt and my underwear, unable to find my nightgowns the night before.

After completing my morning ritual, I made my way downstairs, greeting the other workers as I passed them. Carolyn was at the bottom of the stairs, with clipboard in hand. "Good morning, Sleepyhead," she teased.

"Good morning, Early Bird," I teased back. "What's with all the hammering in the bathroom? You haven't gone wild on me, have you? I was completely serious when I asked that you not spend too much. I will feel such guilt if you do."

Carolyn shook her head. "It isn't that much, like I told you. These are overstock items, and it is no big deal. The only request I have is that you let me reveal the downstairs bath and bedroom to you when they are ready. I can't wait to see the look on your face!"

The phone began to ring, so I went in search of the sound. I found my roll-top desk in what was once the formal dining room. I hoped they would be returning it to the living room; I preferred to have it there. I counted five rings before I was able to open up the desk and retrieve the receiver. "Hello, Wilson residence," I answered.

"Good morning, Miss Wilson. This is Mr. Johnson." I could hear the man's old age in his voice. I covered my exposed ear to drown out the hammering in the back of the house.

"Good morning, Sir. How are you and Mrs. Johnson today?"

"As well as expected, I guess," he responded. "Mrs. Johnson has a desire to buy Ruby Mae's Crown Victoria. Is she still for sale?" I could hear Betty in the background, giving him cues.

"Yes, Sir, it sure is." I was feeling a combination of relief and sadness.

"Wonderful! I am willing to pay your asking price, and prepared to do the deal right away," he said proudly.

"That is terrific, Mr. Johnson. I can't think of anyone better for her car to go to. I am so relieved," I said tearfully. Then I remembered the ticket for the tags that I needed to pay by the end of the month. "Oh, Mr. Johnson, there is one little hitch," I said hesitantly.

"Oh, and what might that be?" He asked.

"I got a ticket for the expired tags last week and need to pay that fine before I can sell you the car. I will take care of that today, sir."

"No need to bother with that. I will take care of it when I pay the sales taxes and register the car. What egg-headed cop would give you a ticket on that car, anyway? You come on over, and we'll complete the deal." With that he clicked off.

I opened the fireproof safe we kept in the bottom drawer and got out the car's title. It would need to be notarized. I remembered that Carolyn was a notary and went to find her.

She was in the downstairs bathroom. I knocked on the door. "Don't come in!" she shouted. I had forgotten about the drama of the big reveal.

"Carolyn, it's me, do you have your notary stamp with you?"

"Yes, it's in my car. Move back into the living room, and I will be right out," she insisted.

I obeyed, but was anxious to get over to the Johnson's house.

She came out in a flurry. "Now, what do I need to notarize?" she asked quickly.

"My neighbors, Mr. and Mrs. Johnson, want to buy the Crown Victoria and I need a notary for transferring the title." There was a plea in my voice.

"Greta, back in a few minutes," she called over her shoulder.

In a moment, we were going down the driveway, Carolyn maneuvering her BMW carefully around all the work vehicles. As we passed the Crown Victoria, parked next to the road and still sporting the *For Sale* sign, I gave her a long look. "She will be in good hands, Grandma." I said out loud. "The Johnsons will take care of her, just like you would."

Carolyn gave me a sideways look of sympathy and peeled out on the road heading to the Johnson's driveway.

We completed our business with Mr. and Mrs. Johnson quickly. I left the keys to the car, the title, and my ticket with them. Before I handed the ticket over, I examined the handwriting of one Officer Garrett. It confirmed that I had actually met him.

It was a nice signature—bold, uniform, and quite legible. I am not a handwriting analyst, but these features spelled honesty, dependability, and intelligence to me. *It's official; I am really out there.*

Carolyn drove back to the house, just as silently and quickly as she had driven out. I was lost in thought, too. Just as she began to turn into the driveway, a gray minivan came barreling over the rise ahead, and she had to slam on the brakes. We slid sideways onto the gravel on the right shoulder. We watched anxiously as the van went off the other side of the road, swerving around Carolyn's front end. The tires screeched and gravel flew away from us. She threw her right arm out to protect me from hitting the dash.

I had caught a glimpse of the driver as the minivan went around us and was shocked to recognize my ex, Bobby Jones. He kept going. I didn't even see the brake lights flash as he passed.

Carolyn and I looked at each other. "Was that...?!" she shouted.

"Uh-huh," I answered, nodding.

"He almost *killed* us!" she screamed.

"I found the green John Deere baseball cap he was wearing very interesting," I said, putting my hands to my red cheeks. "I'm glad the airbags didn't deploy." Sometimes they do more damage than good.

"Maybe you've found your alleged burglar," she commented, cutting the wheel and pulling up off the shoulder. She cautiously turned toward the driveway, driving slowly.

"Possibly, but most of the population of Anderson County wear John Deere hats." I had another thought. "What would Bobby Jones be doing on this side of Clinton this early in the morning? He and Becky live at least an hour's drive away. I find that strange."

"I think it bears some watching," she said with worry. "Remember how violent he was before he left you?" She put the car into its previous space and turned toward me. "Gem, I don't like your being here alone. Please consider getting a roommate or a guard dog for protection."

"There's probably nothing to it. What could he possibly want from me? I haven't even seen him in...well, forever. And besides, he really *is* a coward, a true mama's boy. It's been years! What interest could he possibly have in me now? It's not like I came into money, or something."

"He doesn't know that. Maybe he thinks you have some big inheritance." She arched her eyebrows. "Or maybe he's still angry about something, something unresolved."

"I don't think I meant that much to him. After I lost the baby, he left like a shot and didn't even look back." I didn't want to think about these things. The past has a way of creeping into your life when you aren't expecting it.

"Just the same, I'd be on red alert, if you know what I mean," she insisted.

Whatever the reason for his being in my area, it was working on my nerves. I found him there in the back of my mind the rest of the day. I noticed that Carolyn was jumpy, too. She was snappy with the workers. I gave her looks of comfort when I could. That afternoon, when her husband George came busting through the door, we were both relieved to see him. There is nothing quite like a big strapping man who is sweet as honey to make a girl feel safe.

December 12, 1959

My Brenda Jane was with child. I would not have known except for the bill that came in the mail today from a clinic somewhere in Virginia, marked, For Your Records. In the cause for treatment line it said "pregnancy terminated".

I can't stop thinking on the grand baby I'll never get to hold. Not sure where I went wrong with her. Maybe I'm paying for sins of the past. She had taken to not coming home, but would call as to her whereabouts. I telephoned around and Betty's boy told me he'd heard that she dropped out of school and run off with some folks to California. Maybe she can make a life there and find happiness.

I wish I could have held her one more time and had our goodbyes. I'll keep praying for her and hope she'll come back, someday.

My, but burdens are heavy.
RM

Chapter Thirteen

By Saturday night, the last of the workmen had pulled out of the driveway. The Crown Victoria was nestled into Mrs. Johnson's side of their garage. The weeks since Grandma passed had been a whirlwind of changes.

Carolyn dismissed Greta, and arranged for George to prepare a dinner celebration. He was a great cook, as well as a great accountant. We could smell the stir fry aroma coming from the kitchen as Carolyn and I set the table in the formal dining room.

She had relented and moved my roll-top desk back to the living room, tucked into a cozy niche under the staircase. She had also moved all of my belongings to the master bedroom on the first floor. Her plan was that I would mostly inhabit the bottom floor, saving on electricity—and as a safety precaution; I would be able to exit faster, if an emergency were to occur. I couldn't argue with that logic, especially with the circumstances of late.

She promised to reveal the new look for the master bedroom and the mysterious project that had been going on in the master bathroom after dinner.

She and George made me rest on the back porch while they prepared our dinner. Every few minutes, I would hear one of them giggle and talk in low tones. I couldn't help thinking that a marriage should be exactly that: talking, laughing, sharing. I hadn't experienced any personal examples of relationships between men and women that were successful. *I would like to have something like Carolyn and George have. Is it possible, God?* Could there be a man for me out there who is like George?

If he had any faults, I was yet to see them. George was a very large man, built a lot like Warren Sapp. He had played football in Ohio, where he went to high school, but a knee injury in his junior year ended his chances to play in college. He decided to major in business at the University of Tennessee, where he met Carolyn. His laugh was infectious, and his smile was bright and toothy. No one could be down for long around him; he enjoyed life to the fullest.

We relished our dinner, and laughed over childhood stories that Carolyn and I told on each other. George couldn't believe what juvenile delinquents we were, pulling pranks on the teachers and our classmates. The latter was mostly to get even for their cruelty, the former because they didn't protect or defend us from that cruelty.

I couldn't help but be amazed by how bold I was then. *I don't know if I grew up, or just became passive and beat down. I do know that I am different, but Carolyn is still as much a scrapper as she ever was.*

At dinner, George, being the accountant for Carolyn's business, went over some of the fine points of her meeting with the Flowers at In the Garden. He was going to make it a contractual agreement for a term of three years. Carolyn and I both felt that would be a good time frame.

Finally, with our dessert of rice pudding and coffee under our belts and the table cleared, it was time for the new rooms to be revealed. I felt like a kid on Christmas morning.

Carolyn had me stand at the bedroom door and covered my eyes with her hands until George had the door open. She then uncovered my eyes and yelled, "Surprise!"

A mahogany sleigh bed sat in the middle of the room. It was adorned with a long canopy that came several feet out from the wall and was drawn back on either side, held with large bronze hooks shaped into an oakleaf design. The material was a black and gold pattern of leaves on a cream-colored background. A window seat had been added, padded with a cushion covered in the same material. The throw pillows on the window seat and bed, as well as the curtains, were black and gold. It looked like a room you would see in Buckingham Palace.

"Oh, Carolyn," was all I could choke out.

She clicked on the lights to reveal detailed crown molding and a beautiful chandelier of the same bronze as the canopy hooks. My dresser and chest of drawers were adorned with framed pictures of me and my grandmother, and one of Carolyn and myself at our high school graduation. The wood floor gleamed under gold throw rugs. The whole room glowed. Even George was speechless.

"On to the pièce de résistance," she motioned toward the bath. "The bath has two doors now; one opens from the bedroom, and the other, the original, still opens from the small hallway off the living room."

As Carolyn opened the door a crack, she held up her hand. "Anything you don't like, we can change," she warned.

The bath was a reflection of the bedroom. In the corner to the right sat a garden tub with jets. It was decorated on each side with statues of Venus De Milo and David—miniature versions of the originals, of course. A loin cloth covered David's private area; it matched a ribbon placed on the hair of Venus. I gave Carolyn a look that only another woman would understand. "Is that a necessity?" I asked, pointing at the David statue's covering.

"Yes," she said. "Sometimes a little modesty goes a long way."

Two lighted mirrors adorned two cream-colored sinks, set in a cabinet of mahogany. I pointed to them and looked at Carolyn. She knew what she had done. That was a vanity for a couple. "You never know," she said, smiling.

To the left of the double sinks was a walk-in shower with multiple overhead and wall spouts. *A person could rinse off in a hurry, with all that water spraying in different directions,* I thought.

I looked at the window to find it frosted for privacy but without a curtain. "Are you sure no one can see in?" I asked.

"We tested it; you have complete privacy," she assured me.

The room was accessorized with gold and black linens hung on bronze towel racks, and multiple ferns, some hanging and some on stands. The floor was decorated with gold throw rugs covering cream and black ceramic tiles.

"You like?" she asked.

"I like. You have impressed my socks off." I grabbed her and hugged her.

"Now all you need," she said, smiling up at George, "is someone to share it all with."

George just shook his head and smiled back at her.

April 3, 1965

Got a letter from Brenda today, she is going by "Daisy" now. She is lives in a commune in Washington state. I guess she has become what folks are calling hippies now.

Says she is doing fine, growing her own food and living natural, whatever that means I picture dirt floors and an outhouse like we had in the old days. Just the same, it was good to hear from her.

Thank you Lord,
RM

Chapter Fourteen

After much hugging and enthusiastic appreciation, Carolyn and George left Gem to enjoy her new furnishings.

She wasn't sure what to do first. She walked slowly into her new, elegant bedroom and fell on the bed. Looking up into the canopy, she noticed stars decorated the inside. Carolyn was such a detail-oriented person; it was no wonder that she was so successful and in such demand.

Gem jumped up and started looking through all the drawers for her clothing. Her grandmother's pistol had been placed in the nightstand. She checked to see that it was still loaded, and moved it to the locked drawer in the roll-top desk. It seemed like a logical choice of placement, since it would be both accessible and safe there.

She then threw open the closet door, and there hung her dressy clothes. On the top shelf was a box of Ruby Mae's papers and letters that Carolyn had collected from upstairs. Gem pulled it down and laid it on the bed. Staring at the letters bundled together with ribbons, she suddenly felt as if she were an intruder on her grandmother's life. Gem began to feel gritty and tired, and decided she would take a soothing bubble bath in her new bathroom.

After checking all the door locks and closing all the drapes on the first level, she ran the water for her bath. Measuring a capful of bubble bath, Gem poured it into the stream of water. Her eye was drawn to the frosted glass window, and wondered if Carolyn would be insulted if she added a curtain. She was probably being silly. Carolyn had said that no one could see in, but it would take some getting used to.

Gem undressed and assessed her figure in the mirror. She was very happy with her weight and the toned muscles that her new job had given her. At this point of her life, she was the healthiest, physically, she'd ever been. Mentally, she was very alone and felt anxious about who she was and where she was going, relationship-wise. There was also the nagging thought of her ex being seen so near, and the mystery of who and why someone would want to force their way into the house. Gem also wondered about Mr. Walker's reaction to the diary, and the relationship between him and Ruby Mae.

Sinking slowly into the steamy, soapy water, she looked at the double sinks and mirrors. *Which sink should I use?* It was funny to think that she would possibly someday share this room with someone. There had been very few boys allowed into her grandmother's house, and never beyond the first floor. It was odd to think about a man living in the house. The thought made her giggle.

Gem wished she had put on some music; the house was too quiet. There was no noise other than the sound of her breathing. She decided to cut the bath short. Her mind kept drifting to the box waiting on her bed. She wondered what other secrets it held. Whether it was intruding or not, she wanted to know.

She wrapped her hair into a towel, then put on her comfortable terry-cloth robe and matching slippers. *Carolyn will probably want to make me over next*, she thought. *Honestly, I could probably use it.*

She looked through the letters until she found what she believed was the first one written. It started with *My Dearest Ruby Mae.* It was very informative about the weather, and contained suggestions for doing things around the farm. Henry wrote that he couldn't say where he was stationed and he would write to her again later, when he could. It was signed *Your Loving Husband.*

After reading through several of them, Gem was getting the feeling that her grandfather wasn't terribly romantic. His letters were somewhat bland, and carried very little affection. Yes, times were different then, but this was a man who had just left his bride. *You would think there would be a mention of missing her at some point.* She had soon made it about half way through the bundle of letters, and there was no mention yet of her mother, or when her grandfather would be coming home.

It was late; she would finish the letters another night. *Maybe I should have started with the unopened ones first, but they'll keep.* Placing the ones she had read back in the box, she put the unopened letters that were addressed to Grandpa Henry from her grandma in her night stand. Gem then remembered that she hadn't studied her lesson for Sunday school. She decided she would look at it in the morning, over breakfast.

Gem went to brush her teeth, choosing to use the sink on the right side as hers, imagining "Mr. Green Eyes" on the left side. It just made her more lonesome. With a groan, she flipped off the ornate light switch and climbed into bed, snuggling under the new plush sheets. Staring up at the stars in the canopy, she said a quiet prayer for guidance in approaching a new relationship with a man. "Heavenly Father, if you have someone for me, I think I am ready. I leave it to you, because I know you'll do a better job in picking someone who is right for me. I didn't do such a good job before. Thank you for my friends, and all these beautiful things. I would like someone to share them with, if that is what you want for me. Amen."

During the night, Gem dreamed she was walking through the apple orchard with her grandmother. She was looking up, and the sun was just behind her grandmother's head. Gem couldn't see her face very well and shielded her eyes. "Get you a man that works hard and will treat you right, Gem," she said. "Someone who is not afraid to show his love, someone brave and true."

Gem woke suddenly; sitting up, she looked around in confusion. Her surroundings were unfamiliar; it took a moment before she remembered all the finery that had resulted from Carolyn's efforts, and recognized her new bedroom.

She had heard the voice of Ruby Mae in her dream. It made Gem miss her terribly. She had let her grandmother down by marrying Bobby Jones. *It must have broken her heart too, when things didn't work out.*

If it did, she had never said anything about it to Gem. Ruby Mae sure knew how to keep things to herself. Gem was beginning to see what strength that took.

She settled back into the comfort of her bed and drifted off again, thinking about Ruby Mae's loving words of wisdom. Gem hoped to find someone brave and true, this time.

November 23, 1970

Got another letter from my girl today, she won't be coming for Thanksgiving, again. Haven't set eyes on her in years. Might not even know her if I saw her. Maybe I'm stubborn but I got to keep reaching out. I'm all the people she has and same goes for me.

I'll put pen to paper and hope it reaches her. This one came from Salt Lake City, Utah. At least she's seeing the world.

Thank you Lord for her letter.
RM

Chapter Fifteen

Waking early on Sunday, I decided I didn't want to go to church alone. So, I cooked up a plan. Not wanting to wake anyone too early, I phoned Miss Polly around 9:30 and got the phone number for Calvin's foster family. The foster mother, Mrs. Clark, answered on the seventh ring. She had a cigarettes-and-whiskey voice, very deep and raspy. The call must have gotten her out of bed; she seemed a little disoriented. After I explained who I was and how I knew Calvin, I asked permission to take him to church with me. Mrs. Clark agreed with somewhat of a grunt, and gave me the address. We settled on my picking him up in one hour. It would be too late for Sunday school, but Calvin and I could make church just in time.

After hanging up the phone, I started to have second thoughts. What if Calvin didn't want to go, or I couldn't handle him? He sometimes has autistic episodes, flailing about. Maybe I hadn't thought this though. *It must be time to exercise my faith muscle. Okay, it's you and me God; we can do this, right?*

I took a quick shower in the upstairs bathroom, still a little intimidated by the new modernized shower downstairs. It had so many jets; it might take skin off. I pulled an old but stylish beige suit out of the closet at first, then reconsidered. I thought about what Calvin might be wearing, deciding on a white sweater set and gray skirt instead. After blow drying my hair, I applied mascara and a sheer lip gloss.

The morning had a beautiful summer glow. There was a slight chill in the air, warning that fall was coming. Everything seemed crisp and new. Ladybug turned over like she had been waiting for me. I cracked the window about an inch, and enjoyed the crunching sound of the graveled driveway under the tires.

Heading south out of Clinton, I crossed the Honorable William Everette Lewallen Memorial Bridge toward Claxton. *No disrespect to Mr. Lewallen, but that is a mouthful to call a bridge.* While marveling at the sparkles of sunlight in the Clinch River, slowly rolling westward, I felt a renewed excitement. I breathed in the refreshing air deeply; it was a good day to be alive.

After some searching, I located Calvin's foster home. I'd passed the driveway, quite overgrown with weeds, and needed to turn around. The yard was full of various children's toys and a couple of abandoned cars. A washing machine and a shredded, stained sofa cluttered the small covered porch. The house could best be described as a shack. Peeling white paint showed the previous color of the house, faded past easy identification. It had possibly been a pale green.

Putting Ladybug into neutral and pulling on the emergency brake, I decided to let the engine idle. *This is one place I wouldn't want to be stranded.*

A couple of hungry-looking dogs crawled out from under the porch, barking a greeting or a warning; I wasn't sure which, but I was relieved that they seemed too old to want to jump on me or show much interest beyond sniffing to see if I was friend or foe. The screen door squeaked open as I reached the cinderblock steps.

Before I could speak, a young barefooted man wearing blue jeans and a ripped, dirty t-shirt with profanity on it blocked my path. "You the one pickin' up Calvin?" he slurred.

"Uh, yes," I responded. My mouth had become dry instantly, and my stomach fluttered.

"Wait in the car," he demanded, lighting a cigarette.

I turned slowly and descended the steps. *This environment is unacceptable. The neglect of the yard, the house, and this brassy juvenile delinquent is horrifying.* How could a person with Calvin's limited capabilities be left in such a place?

As I sat waiting in the car, my heart made a decision. *Calvin will not remain in this pigsty.* He deserved something better. *There has to be something I can do...*

Watching as Calvin came out of the house, moving slowly and side-stepping the creep on the porch, I held my breath. As Calvin passed him, the jerk blew smoke right in Calvin's face and laughed. "See ya, Retard," he sneered.

With some difficulty, Calvin made his way down the steps. Jumping out of the car and taking his arm, I put him in Ladybug's passenger seat. He smiled up at me.

"Hi, Miss Gem. I go with you today," he grinned broadly.

"Yes, Calvin," I said comfortingly. "We are going to have a great time today."

If looks could kill, the creature of evil leaning against the door frame would have been dead. He made me feel sick with the look he returned. *He must be demon possessed.*

Without looking back toward the house, I turned the car around in the yard, hoping to not pick up something with the tires and get a flat. Heading down the driveway like a ghost was on my tail, I got a wave of relief when I pulled back onto the road. All I wanted, more than anything, was to be far away from that place and those people.

Looking over at Calvin, I noticed that he was somewhat presentable. His clothes weren't torn or stained, and someone had washed his hands and face—but he smelled like he'd been dried with a soured towel. His hair could have used some work, too. He needed it cut badly.

The church service was everything I had hoped for Calvin. He hummed along with the hymns, and listened intently to Pastor McClendon's sermon. When other worshipers greeted him, he nodded and said, "Hello, Sir" or "Hello, Ma'am." He was very polite and seemed to enjoy himself very much.

We picked up some lunch from McDonald's on our way to the house. Calvin was wide-eyed, watching the food being handed through the window. He touched the bag of warm food like it held a mysterious present. Maybe he had never been to a drive-through before. His whole life was a mystery to me.

When we walked into the house, he turned 'round and 'round, looking at everything, saying "Ooh," and "Oh." We took our food into the kitchen, and I couldn't help thinking about the comparison of where he was living with my house. I wondered how hard it would be to have him taken out of that nightmare, and have him come live with me. *It could happen.* I felt the need to do something about the conditions he is living in. The very least I could do was try.

After lunch, Calvin fell asleep lying on the couch. I didn't have the heart to wake him. I phoned Mrs. Clark and asked if he could stay the night, assuring her that I would take care of him. I started to give a brief explanation, but she agreed before I could complete my argument. *Removing Calvin from there might not be as difficult as I first thought.*

August 4, 1975

Brenda's having a baby. Her last letter came from Oregon.
This one was from California. She seems excited about
being a mother, maybe she is ready now. I pray nothing
happens to her little one. I'm concerned. She didn't
mention a father, or any future plans. Wouldn't it be
wonderful if she came home to have the baby? A mother
can dream you know.

Praise the Lord!
Grandma Ruby Mae

Chapter Sixteen

While Calvin was sleeping, I found some of my old jeans and t-shirts that were stored in the attic. *When he wakes, I will see if he would like to take a shower, so I can launder the clothes he is wearing.* I hoped my hand-me-downs would fit him.

In looking through the attic, I also found some of my grandmother's old bookkeeping paperwork. She was quite the business woman, to make a success of her late husband's farm and raise a child and a grandchild on her own. I was curious to see just how she had accomplished so much.

I had happy memories of raiding the chicken coup for egg money, and harvesting vegetables and fruit to sell to the open-air markets. There were strawberries in the spring, and blackberries at the end of summer. Every season had its opportunity to make money. Fall was time for molasses stir-offs, and winter was for quilt making and crocheting. There was always a job to do on the farm.

Sitting quietly at the roll-top desk with my grandmother's accounting books, I watched Calvin napping. His chest was still rising and falling slowly, showing no signs he would wake soon. He must not have slept well the night before. I cringed to think of him being in that house with a person who was so cruel as to call him Retard as if it was his name, and other things that may have been done to him. Although I hated to contemplate physical abuse, that could explain some of the scars on his arms and his quiet demeanor.

Getting back to the books, I noticed that the newer accounting books were a bright green color. I cracked open the oldest of the book collection, now faded to a pale aqua. It was dated 1948. The rows of assets and liabilities were entered neatly, in Grandma's familiar handwriting.

I could see that she had budgeted for different types of crops and periodic updates, planning to make her farm more modern as the years went on. It must have been very difficult for her to give up most of the land after so many years of struggle and hard work.

The last book was during the years of my leaving the farm to start my life as wife to Bobby Jones. She had already begun to scale back quite a bit on all of her projects. There were no notations of purchases for seeds or equipment, but entries of equipment being sold started to appear. She never really discussed any of these things with me; maybe I was too young, or she wanted me to have something different than being a farmer. Maybe it was because she disliked my marrying Bobby so much.

There was a recurring entry that caught my eye. It was Bobby Jones' name, and the dates were for the years after he divorced me. Every month, she had given him several hundred dollars. I blinked my eyes a few times in disbelief, and looked again as closely as I could. There it was: every month, his name with a payment. *How curious. What could it mean?*

I needed to talk with someone about this right away, so I picked up the phone to dial Carolyn. I then remembered Calvin, asleep on the couch, and went into the kitchen to use the wall-mounted phone there, so I wouldn't wake him. *I really should get a cell phone. I'm so living in the dark ages.*

George answered, saying, "Yellow." He made me laugh.

"Hey George, is Carolyn in?" I asked.

"Sorry, Gem. She is in *Cal-i-forn-i-a*," he said, in syllables. "Is there something I can do for you on this gorgeous Sunday?"

Why couldn't I have married a guy like George? "Maybe, George. Let me run a scenario by you, and you can give me your professional accountant opinion."

"Shoot," he answered.

"Why would a person pay someone a sum of money each month, after they have divorced a relative of theirs? I am talking about several hundred dollars a month, for about two years." I waited, holding my breath, hoping he wouldn't guess that I was talking about my personal issues.

"Well..." I could imagine him rubbing his chin. "It could be a payment for some kind of services...or maybe blackmail, although that would be a stretch. I would really need more information."

"Okay, this is embarrassing, but I would really like to know what you think and I am sure I can trust you." I took a deep breath and let it out slowly. "Ruby Mae was apparently paying Bobby Jones several hundred dollars a month, for a couple of years after we split up." I felt shame and regret.

"Did she know he had become violent?" he asked gently.

"I'm not sure. I was so scared. I tried to hide it from her. When she came to the hospital after I lost the baby, she did ask me if Bobby had done something to make me miscarry. I just shook my head; maybe she didn't believe me. Maybe she paid him to go away, and stay away until I got back on my feet."

"Sounds like Ruby Mae Wilson had lots of secrets. It wouldn't surprise me if she did something like that to protect you," he said comfortingly.

"Thanks, George, you're a peach." I changed the subject. "Guess what? Calvin is here with me today. He and I went to church together, and had lunch from McDonald's. It has been good to have someone else in the house." I chatted on, telling him about Calvin's foster home situation and what I planned to do. I picked his brain a little more about how to take care of Calvin's hair. He suggested I get it cut first, to make it easier to manage, and he mentioned some products that I might purchase.

George promised to fill Carolyn in on everything. He informed me that she would be coming by In the Garden after her flight arrived the afternoon of her appointment. She had several jobs lined up, for all of which she needed materials and plantings.

As I hung up, I pondered the ledger entries concerning my ex, wondering what they meant. It seemed that I had one more thing for which to be thankful to my grandmother.

What a woman! I wish I had paid closer attention. I just thought she was an old lady with an everyday, average life. I wonder what else I don't know about her... I guess we didn't grow as close as I thought during her illness.

May 4, 1976

Brenda's baby was born. March 1st. I'm a Grandma! Wish
I could hold that little baby. I've already missed so much
of her life. What a name she gave her, my goodness I can't
call her all that. I'll think up something. I'm going to sit
down and write her that I'm on my way to see them. Can't
hardly wait to lay eyes on them both.

Thank you Lord for the little miracle.

Your grateful,
RM

Chapter Seventeen

As Calvin was waking from his nap, I sat him up and handed him a glass of water.

"Hello, Sleepyhead." I smiled at him.

He smiled back and drank the whole glass of water in seconds, handing the empty glass back to me. I set it on the coffee table with a soft clink.

"I suppose you need to use the bathroom. It's on the second floor. Come with me, and I'll show you where it is." I held out my hand.

He took my hand and held it all the way up the stairs and down the hall. I showed him where everything was, and asked if he would like to sleep here tonight. He happily nodded. After he had finished in the bathroom, I showed him the room where he would be sleeping, my old room. He went to the bay window like a child runs to the tree on Christmas morning. "Pretty!" he exclaimed at the view of the barn. It looked like a postcard, with the blue Smoky Mountains silhouetted in the background.

I thought, *I must remember to tell Carolyn how he reacted to her decorative touches.* It was as if this room was prepared just for him, with the soft apple-green walls and the top-of-the-world view from the bay window.

"Would you like to go shopping?" I asked, realizing my old clothes were going to be much too big for him.

He just nodded again, still enthralled with the view.

I settled on a sweat shirt and pants set for him to wear.

We headed out to search for a shopping mall that was still open at this time on Sunday afternoons. Calvin's hair needed immediate attention. So, our first stop was as hair salon named *Shear Joy*.

Calvin sat rigid while the hairdresser worked on him. He looked one hundred percent better with his new hairstyle. He wouldn't look directly into the mirror the stylist offered after his cut, but he touched his head repeatedly and smiled.

I noticed the hairdresser checking out my unruly mop, too. "Would you like anything done today?" she asked with a well-meaning smile.

I shook my head. "No, thank you. I'm letting it grow out." Glancing into the wall mirror, I could see why she asked. My hair looked like I had stuck my finger in a wall socket. I tried smoothing it down with my hands, but it just sprang back into its previous state: seriously out of place. *Life changes really take a toll on your hair, apparently.*

For our next stop, we hit the Dollar General Store, where I bought some underwear, socks, jeans, t-shirts, a night light, and hygiene products. I also picked up a few entertaining items for him—a coloring book and crayons, and a hand-held video game. Calvin was thrilled. "I play," he said over and over, patting his new toy as he held it to his chest.

That night, we had soup and sandwiches on the back porch. Calvin helped me with preparing the food, cleaning the kitchen, and washing the dishes. I was once again amazed by his work ethic. He just seemed to have an instinct as to what needed to be done. It made me wonder if he did most of the work at the foster home.

As he was taking his shower, I realized that I had forgotten about pajamas. A t-shirt and gym shorts would have to do. As I pulled his new things out of the dryer, along with the clothes he had worn that day, I realized how much I had missed having another person to do things for. Maybe I needed Calvin as much as he needed me.

With all our preparations for bed completed, we had popcorn and watched *The Wizard of Oz* on DVD. The Scarecrow seemed to be Calvin's favorite; he laughed every time the hay-filled man spoke. When the witch and flying monkeys were on the screen, he turned away. I reassured him, telling him it was just a movie, and patted his arm.

After the movie, I asked if he was ready to go to bed. He nodded while yawning, so I had him brush his teeth and make one more bathroom stop.

As he was climbing into bed, I asked if he would like to say his prayers. He cocked his head to the side and considered my question a moment before agreeing with yet another nod. We did the old standby, Calvin repeating after me: *"Now I lay me down to sleep..."* As I pulled the covers up around him, I saw tears forming in his eyes.

"What's wrong, Honey?" I asked. He just cried harder. I took him in my arms and held him. I couldn't help myself; I began to cry, too.

"Life has turned you around and around, huh?" I said soothingly.

"Miss Gem, I happy," he said between sobs.

"Shh, now, it's okay. I'm glad you're happy. I'm happy, too."

He laughed, and it was like a small bell ringing: a laugh that came from deep inside.

Using my hands, I wiped his eyes and then mine. Taking hold of his shoulders, I looked straight into his eyes. "It's going to be okay," I insisted. "We will have many more days just like this one. You go to sleep now, and if you need anything—anything at all—I am just down stairs. You call me, and I will come running. Okay?"

Calvin nodded, yawning again. "G-night Miss Gem."

"Night-night, Calvin," I answered.

I cut out the light and waited another moment in the doorway before I left him. The room was illuminated by moonlight shining through the window, and I switched on his night light for extra reassurance in case he woke and was scared. In just a few minutes, I heard soft, even breaths, the sound of a person deep in slumber. All seemed right with the world.

I eventually fell asleep, with the nagging memory of seeing Bobby Jones on my road and the entries in my grandmother's ledgers rolling around in my head. Another thought plaguing my mind was how to protect Calvin. *Why didn't I act sooner? I should pay attention to those feelings when I sense them.* I knew the first day I met him that something wasn't quite right. I was too wrapped up in my grief over losing Grandma Ruby Mae and stressed from starting my life over to notice a child with disabilities who was obviously being abused.

May God forgive me, I must do what I can to make it right.

I had one last thought before I dozed off: *When I see Carolyn, I'll ask for her help. She will know just what to do.*

July 4, 1976

The centennial celebration is not in my heart. Not a word
have I heard from my girls. I did get a phone call while I
was in the fields The answering machine plays it over and
over but I still don't know where they might be or when I
might get to see them. Guess I'm learning patience, Lord.

Happy 200th Birthday America
RM

Chapter Eighteen

Waking the next morning, I phoned the school and was informed that it was a day off for students. The secretary called it an in-service day. Calvin and I boogied on into work together. The cooler weather seemed to agree with Ladybug. She was in top form. Bouncing along with the engine humming, we sang at the top of our voices along with the radio, which was playing "I'm a Believer," the Monkees' version. What words Calvin didn't know, he made up with a mumbling sound. We parked in what had become known as my spot, and went into the office for our daily schedule of chores.

Miss Polly greeted us cheerfully. She was looking sharp in a crocheted halter dress, denim jacket, and leather boots. As she handed me the work orders, she leaned toward me with a curious look. "So, how was your weekend?" she asked. "Did you hear from Uncle Ev— I mean, Mr. Walker?"

"No... Should I have?" I had been so busy with Calvin that I hadn't given the protective attention from Mr. Walker last Friday much thought.

"I haven't seen him yet today," she went on, "so I thought maybe his behavior toward you last week might be related." Her arched eyebrows were lifted high.

"No, I haven't heard from him, so the mystery continues." I shrugged.

Calvin was shifting his weight from one foot to the other. I took it as an indication that he was anxious to get to work. "Go on in, Calvin, and get your work apron on. I'll be right behind you," I said, patting his shoulder. He nodded in agreement and shuffled out the side door toward the greenhouse office. I was glad to have a moment alone with Miss Polly.

"I need to contact the Department of Children's Services. The conditions at his foster home are horrible. There's this thug living there that was verbally abusive to Calvin, right in front of me. He can't go back there. He stayed with me Sunday, and was so happy that he cried tears of relief. I have got to do something. I should have done something sooner."

"We have called them, Gem, many times." She shook her head wearily. "The system is so overwhelmed; apparently, it is next to impossible to get his case worker to reverse his placement." She flipped open her Rolodex. "I will give you her number; another try couldn't hurt." She handed me a slip of paper with the information.

"Thanks, Miss Polly. Sometimes, life stinks. What is the penalty for kidnapping in this state?" She responded with a sideways grin.

I put the number in the pocket of my jeans and slipped through the door to catch up with Calvin. I felt defeated already. *Can I really change anything? If I can't get my own life under control, how can I help someone else?*

I passed Jack Flowers on my way to the greenhouses without really noticing him.

"Good morning. Hey, why so distracted?" he asked holding up his clipboard to shade his eyes.

"Sorry... I am just a bit distracted, I guess." I repeated my concerns about Calvin and his living conditions.

"It's tough. But it might help to have someone besides Miss Polly and myself to remind the case worker of his situation. If there is any way that we can help, please let us know." His attention returned to the orders on his clipboard.

I made my way through the rock-walled paths and past Little Eden. As I walked, I was mentally working out my argument for when I would be speaking to Calvin's case worker. I stepped onto the cedar porch of the greenhouse office and heard shouting from inside.

Turning the wrought-iron door handle, I pushed against the door. It wouldn't open; something was blocking it. The shouting inside had turned into shrieked profanities. One of the few words I could make out was "infidel." I ran to the end of the porch and climbed over the rail to get to the side windows. Standing on a pile of river stones, I cupped my hands around my eyes to see inside.

Calvin was lying on the floor, right in front of the door. He wasn't moving. Mr. Walker was struggling with a dark, bearded figure. I had to do something, fast!

The man saw me at the window. I jumped down and started to run toward the front office, grabbing at my side for my walkie-talkie. Failing to find it, I realized it was inside the greenhouse office in my locker.

Suddenly, my arm was grabbed and twisted upward behind me. It was the bearded man, growling words at me in a foreign language. Twisting my arm harder, he dragged me into the greenhouse office. Calvin had been rolled over, away from the entrance. He still wasn't moving. Assessing him head to toe, I saw an injury to his head that was spurting blood to the beat of his heart. He was still alive; *thank you, God.*

Mr. Walker was lying in an awkward position next to the lockers, a bloody shovel beside him. He wasn't moving either.

I looked around the room. A wheelbarrow loaded with ammonium nitrate fertilizer was parked at the half wall to Mr. Walker's office.

Realization came, dimming my fear. *This is the creep who robbed us before!* The fury was rising in my throat. I had to help Calvin and Mr. Walker. I twisted, turned, and kicked, but couldn't get free.

The animal let go of my arm and faced me, choking me with his hands. His black eyes blazed with hate. He lifted and shook my body. He screamed "Die, whore, die!" His hands tightened, cutting my air off.

His odor made me gag. He smelled like a sewer. I tried to kick my dangling legs, but hit only air. I remembered a defensive move I had read about in a magazine. With the heel of my hand, I hit the base of his nose with everything I had. He dropped me to the floor and held his nose, cursing violently. One of the walkie-talkies squawked, "Gem, come in. Over." His ugly head jerked toward the open door. I grabbed the bloody shovel off the top of Mr. Walker and held it high, ready to strike. He spat, barely missing me, and yanked the wheelbarrow out the door.

Dropping the shovel, I made for my walkie-talkie. "Help! Greenhouse office, call nine-one-one, call nine-one-one!" I then ran for Calvin. Taking my bandana out of my pocket, I covered his head wound with it and applied pressure, hoping to stop the bleeding.

Mr. Walker moved his legs and looked over at me. "Is that you, Ruby Mae?" he asked weakly. Before I could reply, I heard pounding footsteps. Suddenly the room filled with people, all of them asking me questions too fast for me to answer. The only thing I wanted to hear was the siren of an ambulance. Calvin began having a seizure. Unable to keep hold of his head, I began to shake all over. I heard a moaning sound, like the wail of a wounded animal. A few seconds later, I realized it was coming from me, but I couldn't stop. I had flashes of Bobby coming at me with his fists, and of Calvin crying as I held him.

An EMT swabbed my arm with something cold and stuck a needle in me. I welcomed the soft darkness as it folded around me.

December 24, 1976

My Christmas wish is to hear from Brenda and to know
that she and the baby are well. Someone once said that
life isn't fair. I'd like to hit them in the nose with my jingle
bells. Not a Christian thing to think, I suppose I'd like to
have family around me this lonesome time of year.

Not So Merry,
RM

Chapter Nineteen

I opened my eyes. They felt dry and full of grit, and my lips were stuck together. I tried to focus on my surroundings. I was obviously in some type of medical facility, wearing a hospital gown and in a room with a sliding curtain with hooks.

A sweet, round, unfamiliar face appeared in the opening. "How are we doing?"

I answered with a squeak, "Okay, thirsty." Before I could ask about Calvin and Mr. Walker, she disappeared again. I flashed back, seeing Calvin lying there with his head bloody and shaking all over in a seizure, his jaws clamped tight. *I've got to get to him. I wonder where they took him. I wonder where I am.*

The nurse popped back in with a pitcher of ice water and a plastic cup. "Here you go, Sweetie," she said, handing me the cup. *I am not her sweetie,* I thought muzzily. I drank the water. It was cold enough to make my throat ache, and tasted metallic.

"Where were the others, Calvin and Mr. Walker, taken?" I insisted before she could disappear again.

"I'm not sure who you are talking about. I just came on my shift. They tell me you were pretty hysterical, and they needed to sedate you. You have some nasty bruises on your neck. We needed to observe you for complications. What happened to you?" She tilted her head to the side as if she were settling in for a good story to tell the other nurses at break time.

"If you will just take these tubes out of my arm, I need to leave." I didn't have time to entertain her.

Carolyn came shooting around the corner. I was never so relieved to see anyone. She proceeded to shoo the busybody nurse out of the room, and took over my care. Examining my throat, she shook her head. I cough. My throat was so dry. I downed another cup of water so I could speak to her.

"Get me out of here! I need to get to Calvin. What about Mr. Walker?"

"What, no hello for me?" she teased.

"Okay, hello Carolyn, it is wonderful to see you. How have you been?" I gave her my best fake smile. "Now get me out of here!"

"Relax please; it's just the emergency room. They haven't admitted you. I'll go find your doctor and see if you are ready to be released. As for Calvin, they airlifted him to UT Medical Center, and Mr. Walker is just across the aisle. He was knocked unconscious, but seems to be recovering."

I nodded that I understood. She acknowledged the nod with a wink and glided back through the curtain to find the ER doctor.

I wonder if Calvin knew he had ridden in a helicopter to the hospital. I recalled his reaction when one flew over while we were working. When he heard the sound of the blades, he waited for it to appear. His eyes followed it until the chopper disappeared over the horizon. He looked at me and said two words, "Whoop whoop," emulating the sound of the blades. *I should take him for a helicopter ride. They still have those in Pigeon Forge, where you get a tour over the Smoky Mountains. That would be terrific.*

After the ER doctor gave me a page of instructions, the nurse removed my tubes and I got dressed. Carolyn had brought a change of clothing for me. She casually said that the clothes I was wearing had been discarded. What she didn't say was that they were covered with Calvin's blood. The thought of all that blood made me swoon a little, but I fought it because I needed to get to Calvin.

As we passed the curtain where Mr. Walker was being treated, I caught a glimpse of Miss Polly sitting by her uncle's bedside, holding his hand. I gave her a little wave, and she motioned me inside. Carolyn said she would bring the car around to the entrance and wait for me. I patted her arm and nodded.

"How is he?" I asked Miss Polly.

"He's going to be okay. He was awake for a while, but there were some concerns about his blood pressure, so they sedated him. He kept asking about you and Calvin." She was holding back tears. Her pretty, expertly made-up eyes were terribly red.

"When he wakes again, tell him I'm fine, and I am off to see about Calvin."

"Oh, Gem, I almost forgot. Jack has talked with the authorities, but they want to ask you some questions, too, when you are able. It seems that this type of crime is considered a terrorist action, and the big dogs have been called in." She folded her arms and her lips became a thin line. "It means that we will become a media circus for a while."

"I hadn't thought of that. Well, if they want to find me, tell them I will be at UT Med Center." I took one last look at Mr. Walker. He looked so different with his face relaxed and still: almost nice. I squeezed Miss Polly's hand and headed out to where Carolyn was waiting in her BMW.

As soon as I slid into the passenger seat, she took off. Mario Andretti would have been proud of the speed and maneuvering with which she drove. I began to suspect that she wanted to get there as badly as I did. We spoke very little; she was concentrating on her driving, and I on praying for Calvin. He needed a familiar face there when he woke up. I also wondered about the foster family. Had someone called them?

As Carolyn parked the car in the visitor's lot, she turned to me. "If anything happened to you, I would lose my mind. I am so glad you are all right."

"Same here, and thank you for rescuing me. You must have flown home early. I hope that didn't cost you a job. I don't know what I would do without you in my life."

"There's nowhere else I would want or need to be," she said flatly. "We are going to get through this, together."

I seem to be surviving a lot of things lately, I mused. *I hope to say the same for Calvin.* We scurried into the hospital and made a beeline to the information desk.

September 5, 1981

Not celebrating Labor Day this year. We have had so much
rain, we have food rotting on the vine. Will take a day off
when the harvest is in and my people are paid. Seems to be
harder every year to get the crops to market. Our economy
is changing, so is our little country town. Everybody wants
fast food now.

It's a confusing time for me.
RM

Chapter Twenty

Calvin was still in the critical care unit. Carolyn and I were stopped at the nurse's desk. Apparently, only one person at a time is allowed in these rooms, and it's usually only family members. After a short explanation about Calvin's background, they agreed to let us see him. Carolyn signaled me as the one to go into the restricted area. I went as quickly as I could move, without hesitation. I needed proof that he was still alive.

A nurse led me to his room. He looked like a small child in the bed. He was so still. Machines were pumping and beeping. He had tubes in his arm, nose, and mouth. I counted three IV bags: one with blood, one with an antibiotic, and one with a glucose and electrolyte solution. His head was bandaged. Both eyes had black half circles under them. There was a heavy scent of chemicals in the air.

Standing over him, I held his hand. "Please God" I prayed, "give him a chance at some happiness before you take him. Please." The room blurred as tears pooled in my eyes. "This can't be it for him. We have so much to do, so much fun to have, so much to laugh and learn about."

The same nurse came in moments later. "I am sorry, but you will need to leave now."

I wiped my face with my hands. "He really has no one. Please come and get me when he wakes up. I want him to see someone he knows, so he won't be afraid." I searched her face for understanding.

"I'll make a note on his chart. Are you a relative?" she asked.

"No, but I would like to be. He is such a terrific kid, really special."

She took down my name. "If you will go wait in the lounge; I will see that you are notified of any change," she assured me.

Reluctantly, I backed out of his unit, still searching his face for any sign of movement. "Please hang on, Calvin. I will be right here," I said as I touched his foot.

Turning down the hallway, I felt an overwhelming sense of grief. *So much loss; I can't lose him too, not just when we were starting to know each other. Come on God, work a miracle here. Oh yeah–if it be your will.* Pastor McClendon was always reminding us of trusting that God knew best for us. *Please, let it be your will.*

The waiting room was full of people and their belongings. Scattered around the room were personal bed pillows of various colors, and half a dozen overnight bags. These people were all waiting for either very good or very bad news, and I was to become one of them. Some were talking softly to each other, some sleeping in reclining chairs, others crying silently.

Carolyn and I gave the attendant lady, clothed in a cheerful, yellow flowered smock, our names and the name of our loved one who was in ICU. She was well past retirement age and showed a natural ability for compassion and assurance, patting my arm and nodding sympathetically. I couldn't help wondering if she had been required to apply for this volunteer position. I imagined some of the questions that would have been a part of the interview. *Do you handle stressful situations well? Are you sympathetic to the grief and suffering of others? Can you remain patient and cheerful when others are falling apart?* She looked to me like someone who would be smiling and uplifting even if the room were on fire.

Carolyn and I made our way to a row of empty recliners on the far side of the room. Fortunately, they were next to the windows. Unfortunately, they were too far away from the attendant's desk to get news quickly. I wondered why I felt angry toward her. She was just doing her job. When her desk phone rang, the whole room came to attention and the edge of their seats. "Henderson family," she called out.

Two ladies put their purses on their arms and walked to her desk. Words were spoken softly to them and they stepped out into the hall. Carolyn and I proceeded to make ourselves comfortable. She started reading a decorating magazine, while I stared out the window and thought about the way Calvin laughed that morning at the sound his cereal made. "Pop, pop," he had snickered, leaning his ear toward the bowl.

The two ladies came back into the room. It was obvious that their loved one had not recovered. Their faces were drawn. One stood, leaning against the wall while the other one gathered their things. The lady in yellow helped them, and repeated how sorry she was several times. After they had exited, she removed their discarded coffee cups and food wrappers. The spot was now ready for the next anxious person to occupy.

George popped his head in the door and spied us. He gave the attendant two thumbs up and strolled on by her. Making three large strides, he was across the room, hugging us both. "What can I do? Anything you need, name it."

"There's really nothing to do but wait. His doctor should let us know his prognosis soon. They know we are here," I said, sounding like a robot.

Carolyn left to go get us some food. I had no appetite but didn't argue, knowing she needed to be busy. George tried to take my mind off things by making small talk about me, the house, and his business. They say you can tell who your friends are when there is a tragedy. I had never wondered that about George and Carolyn, if they were true friends. *In that, I'm so blessed.*

Carolyn returned with coffee and sandwiches. I took a bite of egg salad and chewed on it, but couldn't convince my throat to swallow. I washed it down with the bitter coffee. She and George made scheduling plans for being at the hospital with me. Time seemed to crawl by. *I wonder if they will let me see Calvin again.*

The magic phone rang once again. The elderly volunteer, sitting calmly at her desk answered, "ICU lounge." The room held its breath as she listened. "Thank you," she responded to the mystery caller. "Wilson, Gem Wilson," she called out.

We made our way to the desk. "The doctor will see you now. Just down the hall and on your left." She smiled cheerfully. I couldn't tell if it would be good or bad news. Her demeanor was always the same. I wanted to grab her and shake it out of her, but I gritted my teeth and said nothing.

Making our way down the hall, we entered a small room with a rectangular table and folding chairs, but we didn't sit. The doctor was standing at the table's far edge, juggling many things. He had a pocketful of pens, as well as one behind his ear. He was wearing a pair of wire-rimmed glasses on his shiny, bald head, and black plastic ones on his pug nose. A stack of patient's charts was in his arms. He began to read from the top one, saying, "I understand the situation with Calvin and the lack of family. Otherwise, I wouldn't be speaking with you." He leaned his head back, looking down at us. Feeling we were worthy of his information, he continued. "We will be moving Calvin to another room. He hasn't shown a great deal of improvement, but there have been no diminishing signs. He is breathing on his own, and his vital signs are normal. He can be properly monitored in the step-down unit, and is no longer in eminent danger." He closed the chart. "Are there any questions?" He said it as if he dared us to ask any.

"What are his chances?" I asked, folding my arms in a defiant stance.

"The next twenty-four hours will tell," he stated. "He could recover to the level he was before, or he could have irreversible brain damage. We won't know until he is fully conscious."

He paused a moment, letting that sink in. When we didn't say anything else, he nodded his goodbye and bounded out the door and down the hall.

"Well!" Carolyn said. "That was short and not so sweet."

"Let's find out what room they're moving him to," I responded. "These hospital employees are obviously just going through the motions. I want to focus on making sure Calvin has what he needs for every chance to recover."

December 31, 1982

It is going to be a very Happy New Year! Got a letter from Brenda today. She is coming for a visit and bringing the baby. I have decided to call her Gem.

I am finally going to be a real grandma. Good things come to those that wait, or maybe even a blind squirrel comes across a nut sometimes I don't care, I just feel so blessed right now.

Thank you, Jesus!
RM

Chapter Twenty-one

We waited and watched as Calvin was rolled into his new room. There were still no signs of movement. The nurses moved his bed into position and hooked up his oxygen and monitors.

"Why is there an oxygen tube in his nose?" I asked. "I thought he was breathing on his own."

"He is, but it helps him to breathe more fully. If the alarm should go off, we will know that there is a problem. It's a precautionary measure," said the older nurse.

She and the other nurse wrote their names on the erasable board attached to the wall across from his bed. One was named Brandi, the other July. I couldn't help wondering if that was pronounced as Julie, or like the month. Before I could ask, a surprise was standing at the door. This had to be the foster mother.

Her snow-white hair was in a bun, with loosened strands falling around her withered face. She was bent and shriveled. She had not aged well. Her lips were drawn in a permanent frown, and she carried a cane in her gnarled hand. Her eyes were flat and mean like a shark's. She seemed more irritated than concerned.

"So," she addressed the nurses, "what's to come of him? Will he make it?" Her scratchy, cigarettes and whiskey voice was as I remembered from the phone call I had made to her only yesterday. It seemed as if it were long ago.

As the nurses filled her in on his prognosis, she nodded with the occasional grunt.

"Do everything you can. I need him to live," she instructed them.

She then turned her attention to us. "What are YOU people doing here?"

Carolyn and I approached her. "What do you mean, you need him to live? That's an odd response after what he has been through," Carolyn said, getting fired up. "Maybe it's his government check you need. It's not like you spend it on his hair, teeth, or decent clothes for *him*."

I looked over at Calvin. "Let's step into the hall." The foster mother ignored me.

"Who do you think you are? This is my charge. I am responsible for him." She shook her crooked finger at us.

I stepped toward her and spoke in a pronounced whisper. "We are people who care about Calvin. I saw the environment you provide, and the type of people that live there. Calvin deserves better. Shame on you!" I said, raising my voice.

"I don't have to stand here and take this from you nobodies." Turning to the nurse, she said, "I will leave my information at the desk. I am to be informed of any change. I'd like these people removed, *immediately!*" With that she turned and stomped out, her cane whacking the floor hard with each step. She didn't look back.

Carolyn and I looked at each other and shook our heads. The nurses shrugged their shoulders. It was obvious that they weren't going to kick us out.

George, ever the calm in any storm spoke. "Has anyone called his case worker?"

Carolyn sprang into action. "No time like the present." She took off toward the door to make the call.

"Carolyn," I called to her. "Will you call Pastor McClendon too, please?"

She hesitated, but nodded an okay.

George and I moved the two reclining chairs to the edge of Calvin's bed and made ourselves as comfortable as possible. Watching the rise and fall of

Calvin's chest, I felt myself nodding off.

There was a rap at the door. I blinked my eyes to be sure of what I was seeing. There stood Officer Garrett. "May I come in?" He was dressed in blue jeans and a white button-down shirt. Out of uniform, he looked like Robert Redford from *The Sundance Kid.*

I quickly glanced at Calvin. No change. "Yes, please do."

George looked at our visitor, and then looked at me. "I think I'll stretch my legs and see how Carolyn is doing." He gave me a knowing look and nodded at Officer Garrett.

"Officer Garrett, George Woodward," I introduced them and they mannerly shook hands, both saying, "Nice to meet you." George then slid out the door.

"What is your first name?" I surprised myself with my boldness.

"It's Jeremy. Jeremy Garrett, and yours?" He crossed the room and sat in George's vacant seat. He looked at the bruises on my neck.

I touched my neck and swallowed hard. "My name is somewhat embarrassing." I couldn't believe I was sitting here talking with him like an old friend. "It was given to me by my hippie mother. I shortened it to Gem. My grandmother suggested it would be best to have a name that others could understand. But my real name is—are you ready? Brace yourself; it's Gemini Rainbow Wilson." I waited for him to laugh.

"Wow! That is quite a name. My middle name is Johnson. Can you imagine? Jeremiah Johnson Garrett. For someone who resembles the actor who played that character in that movie, it was a hard act to follow. And then there was the initial thing; it was all I could do to keep them from calling me J.J." He smiled and his green eyes twinkled.

I began to tell him my life story. I told him the tale of living in the commune, my mother's abandonment, loss of my marriage and my baby, and losing my grandmother. I opened up to him with no thought of consequences or fear. I finished with the mystery of my strange relationship with Mr. Walker, and the strong one with Carolyn and George. I was feeling very light hearted by then, as if a burden had been lifted from my shoulders.

"I came here to see how you and Calvin were. I have some information for you about your attacker." His face became solemn. "We have him in custody. Your statement is needed. Since Calvin is unable and Mr. Walker is still under sedation, it's up to you."

"I can't leave him." I shook my head.

He looked at Calvin and then at me. "I understand. It would be good if they came to you."

"How was the guy arrested? Did he hurt anyone else?"

"No. The department has had In the Garden staked out since the first robbery. We got him as he fled for a waiting minivan parked in the emergency shoulder on the interstate. He was caught red-handed with the stolen fertilizer. The van had all the other ingredients needed to build quite a lot of explosives. Still, an eyewitness would tie things up nicely."

"This van, it doesn't happen to be gray and belong to one Bobby Jones, does it?" I held my breath.

"No, it was a white van." He gave me a curious look.

"Good, okay." I didn't offer any explanation and to my relief, he didn't ask any further questions.

"I will talk to the higher ups on the force and see about setting up a visit so you won't have to leave Calvin. My superiors were supportive when I requested to see you. Hopefully, they will continue to be generous." He reached to pat my shoulder and instead took my hand. Pulling a card from his shirt pocket, he placed it in my hand. "Here's my personal number," he said, smiling into my eyes. When he let go of my hand, I missed his touch immediately. He looked over Calvin. "Hang in there, Little Buddy." He whispered.

He slowly backed out of the room as if he were reluctant to leave. As he disappeared out the door, he held his hand up in a goodbye gesture.

"Well, Calvin what do you think about that?" I asked, waiting for a response.

He slept on.

March 1, 1983

My granddaughter is so beautiful. It was love at first sight.
I've missed so much of her childhood. She's a towhead with
the biggest blue eyes I ever saw.

I look forward to teaching her all I know.

As we celebrate her 7th birthday today, I'm trying not
think on how quiet Brenda is being and jumpy.
It's like she's afraid of something.

She has no answers for the time she's been gone, it's all so
odd. None of that can take away my joy at having my
grandbaby here.

Oh happy day!
Ruby Mae

Chapter Twenty-two

Carolyn and George returned, talking close and low. They both had Cheshire cat grins. As they took a seat, Carolyn began to question me about Jeremy Garrett's visit.

"What did he say? What did you say? Will you see him again?" She was firing them at me more quickly than I could possibly answer them.

"Slow down." I put my hands up to signal a pause. "He was here to see about us, and to let me know that the attacker had been arrested."

She looked disappointed. "But," I continued, "we had a very long talk and got to know a lot more about each other." That seemed to please her.

The alarm on Calvin's oxygen monitor sounded. It was deafening. We all jumped to our feet. His nurse, July, popped into the room. She checked him and the monitor. "False alarm," she said. "Sometimes that happens if the patient isn't breathing deeply enough."

Still, it had scared the wits out of me. George and Carolyn looked shaken, too.

The phone rang, and I answered it. "Hello."

"Miss Wilson?" said a deep, serious voice.

"This is she," I responded.

"Special Agent Cochran, FBI. We need to meet with you as soon as possible at the Anderson County Hall. Your eyewitness account of the terrorist incident is crucial." He was very businesslike.

"Look, I need to be here when Calvin wakes. If you wish to speak with me, you will need to come here." I couldn't be that important. They had the evidence and the criminal. Why is talking with me so crucial?

"We are sending guards, protection for you and Calvin. The officer will then escort you to meet with our agents. We feel that there is an organized group involved in the crime. I apologize, but I can't give you much information. I can tell you that the man we have in custody was expendable to them, but because of newspaper and media reports, they know about the victims: you, Calvin, and Mr. Walker." He waited my response.

"What?" I gripped the receiver. George, sensing my distress, took over the conversation.

I looked at Carolyn. "They're sending guards. They feel that we are still in danger. The paper, TV, they reported the crime. Do we have a paper?" I was shaking.

"No, but I will get one for you. Also, Gem, I wasn't able to reach Calvin's case worker, so I left her a message. Pastor McClendon is on his way." She patted my arm. "Here, sit down and try to stay calm. I'll see what I can find out. Back in a flash." She dashed out.

George finished the phone call and rubbed his chin, his thinking gesture. "Gem, I'm afraid you will need to talk to these men. It has become a national security situation. I will go with you, if you like."

"I will not leave Calvin," I insisted.

The phone rang again. George answered it. "Hello". He paused and listened. He looked at me and covered the receiver with his hand. "It's a reporter. You don't want to talk to him, do you?" It was more a statement than a question. I shook my head no. "Sorry, Dude, she has no comment at this time." As soon as he disconnected, the phone rang again.

"Hello... Really?" His eyebrows went up. "How can I be sure you are who you say you are?" he asked the caller. He listened for a moment, and his mouth fell open. "It's your mother, Gem." He held out the receiver to me.

I shook my head and covered my ears. "No. What? No. I can't. No," was all I could say.

He made an excuse that I was indisposed, and requested she call back later. He then reached down and unplugged the phone.

"Calvin and I are having a very interesting day, aren't we?" I said, taking his hand. I didn't know whether to laugh or cry. "I wonder what the rest of the world is hearing about the attack. Should we turn on the TV? No, Calvin will hear. They say that people who are unconscious still hear things. We will wait for Carolyn to bring the paper." I seemed to be frozen in place. So, my mother was alive and she remembered that she had a daughter. Some organized terrorist group was out to finish what their man started. What next?

March 6, 1983

Just like that, Brenda's off again, disappeared into the
night. Would have thought she might have learned to
say goodbye by now. Don't know what's wrong with that
girl, thought I'd raised her better than that. She left
Gem with me.

The child doesn't seem too upset. Says that her Momma is
always leaving her with folks but comes back. So, I guess
me and my little Gem will make the best of it. She's such
a quiet child, never makes a fuss. Guess she has learned to
do without. Guess I'm getting a second chance at raising a
girl, please Lord, let this one turn out better.

Fretfully,
RM

Chapter Twenty-three

Carolyn returned with the newspaper. We read the headline, printed all in caps: *TERRORIST ATTACK AT THE GARDEN OF EDEN*. It sounded like a strange Bible story. The reporter had covered information from the first robbery attempt to the details of the attack in the greenhouse. It gave all the names of the victims, where we all lived, and at what hospitals we had received treatment. The reporter was so thorough that he had created the need for us to have a guard. In our situation, freedom of the press took away the freedom of the people involved.

In the early afternoon, two burly men wearing earphones and wrist mics came in to introduce themselves. They said their names, but I was having trouble remembering them. Pete, Paul, Mark, Mike? I wasn't really listening. Calvin had developed a fever, and it was all I could think about. The nurses were beginning to look concerned also.

Feeling that I was in good hands for the moment, Carolyn and George left. They needed to take care of some things with their respective businesses. They promised to drop back by later in the evening. Carolyn couldn't resist reminding me to pace myself, ever the protector, looking out for me.

My next visitor was a bit surprising. Calvin's caseworker showed her identification at the door to gain entry. She was young, a recent graduate of the University of Tennessee College of Social Work. *I imagine her degree is so new that it hasn't even been framed yet.* She was quite slim and very blonde. Her name was Gloria Swan. She was obviously terribly inexperienced, and a bit nervous.

I introduced myself as Calvin's co-worker and friend. She seemed genuinely glad that he had a friend. She informed me that she would be taking over as Calvin's caseworker. The previous one had just retired and all of her cases had been reassigned.

"May I tell you of his history?" she asked, wide eyed.

"Yes, I am very curious about his history." I was on the edge of my seat. "But, should we be talking in front of him? He can hear us, you know." I rubbed his hand.

"It wouldn't be something he doesn't already know." She shrugged.

She pulled a file from her brand new, shiny briefcase. "As an infant, he was left at the hospital emergency door. He was apparently a victim of shaken baby syndrome. In other words, someone had abused him and abandoned him. He had no last name, but was wearing Calvin Klein baby shoes. Therefore, he became known at the hospital nursery as Calvin Doe." She stopped for a moment, and searched my face to see if I was ready for her to go on.

A little more relaxed, she continued. "He was placed in a foster home at an estimated age of three months old. It was hoped that the family would adopt him. At the age of two, they realized that he would need a lot of therapy and surgeries to have anything close to a normal life, because of the brain injuries he had suffered at the hands of his birth parent or parents. They were not prepared to deal with all of that. He went back into the system and was placed in an orphanage. At the age of ten, he was placed in his current home. The agency suspects that the foster mother wants him there for the monthly checks she receives. Sadly, that is a situation that happens more often than it should. It is also one that is very hard to prove. The alternative would be a group home, or returning him to the orphanage. It is hard to decide which are the lesser of two evils."

"So, you have a record of the calls from Mr. and Mrs. Flowers, about his treatment by his present placement?" I felt myself becoming hopeful.

"Yes, but we don't have a lot of choices here. Say I do remove him.

Where is he to go from there?" she asked.

"To me, I want him. I would love to take care of him. He is a joy to me. Calvin is such a wonderful human being. His laugh is the most beautiful sound. He expects so little, and is grateful for every little thing. I would welcome the responsibility of his needs. I love this boy, so much." I hadn't realized the depth of what he meant to me until just that moment.

"That's good news." She smiled. "It gives me something to work with. The only problem I can see is all the media coverage surrounding you right now." She shrugged. "Hopefully, things will die down soon and get back to normal." She had the type of enthusiasm that comes with starting a new job. With her as his caseworker, I felt I had a chance at keeping Calvin.

I thanked her for coming, and she promised to stay in touch about his case and removing him from his current placement. She left pamphlets about adoption and becoming a foster parent for me to look over.

After she left, I leaned in to Calvin. "Did you hear all that? Would you like to come home with me forever? You've got to wake up first. Come on Calvin, wake up baby. Please, wake up." He didn't even stir. I sighed and sat back in the vinyl recliner.

The nurses came in to change his fluids and check his vitals. At their suggestion, I reluctantly took myself to the restroom and walked down the hall to the lounge for some coffee. The television was on in the lounge. I saw a picture on the screen of me, then one of Calvin, and finally Mr. Walker. Mine looked like my driver's license, ugh. Calvin's was from his employee of the month picture at work. He had a proud grin. Mr. Walker's was very different from the man I know; he was smiling. Then up came a picture of the man they had arrested. He looked insane and unruly. It was obviously his mug shot. The news anchor was talking about the history of Oak Ridge, and the Manhattan Project from World War II. He went on to tell about the robbery and arrest. Surprisingly, there was a car chase between local officers and the alleged terrorist. They also spoke of the evidence, plans that were found to bomb many government buildings and laboratories in Oak Ridge. They felt that In the Garden nursery was targeted because of its close access to the interstate. They went on to say that two victims had been released from the hospital, but one remained in critical condition.

Since this was the national news, I suppose that is why my mother came out of the woodwork. I really didn't know how to react to her. *I wonder if she knows that Grandma Ruby Mae is dead. I wonder what continent she called from this time.* It had been many years since she had sent me a birthday card—and even more since she had last called, as far as I knew. Ruby Mae had a lot of secrets. Maybe some of them involved my mother.

July 1, 1993

The crop is good this year. If the rain holds out, we will have the best crop since I took over the farm. Got to brag on my Gem, she's quite the farmer. Nothing gets by her. She seems to notice every need and how to meet it.

Her being a teenager hasn't been the nightmare I encountered with her mother. She's such a special girl and becoming a terrific young woman. Only troublesome thing, she's seeing a boy, a troublemaker. I'm hoping that it passes

Watch over my girl, Lord.

Prayerfully,
RM

Chapter Twenty-four

Hospitals take on a different vibe at night. All seems so still, yet the night staff is buzzing around, periodically waking patients to check on them and take their vital signs.

Calvin's temperature was still high, but it hadn't gone above 102 degrees. His nurses for the night shift were saying very little. They came into the room, checked monitors, fluids, blood pressure, and temperature. Then they softly stepped out.

The guards were on a rotating schedule. One was always present, just outside the door. I didn't know how they could stand in one place so long, staring into space.

Carolyn had come by with a change of clothes and a basket of food for me. She didn't stay long because it was so late, but she promised to relieve me in the morning.

I found myself dozing off and on in the chair. As I sat rubbing Calvin's arm, I fell asleep with my head next to his shoulder. The darkness had engulfed me. I released all worry and surrendered to it.

A movement woke me. Were the nurses back in the room? They had just left. Maybe it was Pastor McClendon. He had yet to show up. I raised my heavy head to see Calvin looking at me. His eyes half open, he opened and closed his mouth slowly.

"Oh! Calvin!" I sat straight up. "Welcome back. It is so good to see you awake. Let's call the nurse." I reached for his call button.

He smiled at me. I reached above his head and hit the button. "Yes," Answered a complacent voice.

"He's awake!" I exclaimed.

"Be right there," she responded flatly.

Calvin smiled on. Suddenly a frown crossed his forehead, wrinkling his bandage. I took hold of his hand. He raised the index finger of his free hand. "Look, Miss Gem, angels."

"What?" Did I hear him right?

"Angels," he repeated, pointing at the wall across from his bed.

There was a painting on the wall, but it was of a sunflower field. Maybe he was hallucinating. Maybe he saw the shape of an angel in the painting.

He looked away from the wall and looked me in the eye. It was like he was looking inside me. He looked sad, and his eyes watered. I smiled at him. "It's going to be okay, Calvin," I assured him.

"Angels are here," he stated as if he were trying to convince me.

Where are those nurses? What could be taking so long?

"I love you, Calvin. And if you think you see angels, then, I am sure that they are there." I gripped his hand and smiled, hoping it would keep him calm.

Suddenly he squeezed my hand very tight, and his eyes rolled back into his head. His body began to shake violently, pulling my arm back and forth with it.

I reached behind him with my free arm and pushed the call button again. There was no response. Calvin kept rocking back and forth. He had a vice grip on my hand. A blaring ring filled the room as his monitors all went off at the same time. He was gnashing his teeth together. His face was twisted in a grimace of pain. His feet and hands were curling inward. Every muscle and limb had become contracted and stiff.

"Oh, Calvin, baby, hang on, hang on, help is coming," I repeated over and over.

Finally, after what seemed like an eternity, a gaggle of medical help burst through the door. "He wouldn't let us in." One of them gestured toward the guard.

They took over, yelling commands. They wanted me to go to the hall, but I couldn't remove my hand from Calvin's grip. I shook my head as if to say I'm sorry, pointing at his hold on me.

As quickly as it had begun to shake, Calvin's body relaxed totally. He breathed in deep through his mouth and exhaled. I felt his life force leave with the breath.

"No!" I screamed. I looked at the room full of the medical personnel, searching each face for an answer. The heart machine, which had been keeping time with my own since yesterday, flatlined.

Pushing me aside, they began CPR. It was all a blur through my watering eyes. The doctor was counting compressions, and the nurse gave him air by squeezing a large plastic bulbous contraption she fitted over his face. After what seemed like an eternity, the nurses and the doctor started shaking their heads. The doctor looked at his watch. "I'm calling it. Time of death, two twenty-one a.m."

I looked down at Calvin. He had the same peaceful expression I had seen on my baby boy as I had held him for the first and last time, and my grandmother as she drew her last breath. His life on earth was over.

"I don't understand," I cried out. "Why? Oh, Calvin. No." I looked at the doctor, hoping for some answer.

"We did all we could. I'm sorry for your loss." He gave my arm a comforting pat. "We need to work in here for a while to remove all the equipment and prepare him. Would you like to stay? Is there someone we can call for you?" He looked at me compassionately. All I could manage was an unbelieving head shake.

I picked up Calvin's dangling hand and placed it on the bed. As I bent over to kiss his still warm cheek, my tears fell on his nose. I wiped them off with my hand. I picked up my purse, gave him one last look, and slowly backed out of the room.

At the nurse's desk, I asked for a piece of paper. On the paper, I wrote the following words. Words that I could barely see through my tears.

Please release Calvin's body to me. I wish to give him a proper burial.
Gem Wilson

I handed the note back to her. "Please see that the foster mother gets this note. I am sure she will be relieved to forgo any financial responsibility." She nodded in understanding.

I went into the lounge to call Carolyn, and changed my mind. She would be sleeping. *Bad news can wait until the morning. Where is Pastor McClendon? Him, I can call.*

In the lounge, I found the phone to be one with the old style rotary dial. Watching the dial return to its position with each turn was hypnotic. I felt like I was grabbing at a life line. "Please be there." My hand was sore where Calvin had squeezed it during his seizure.

"Hello," he said, his voice mellow. I could hear old age in it I hadn't noticed before.

"Pastor, it's Gem. Calvin didn't make it. I need you. Can you come?" My voice was almost a whisper; I wondered if he had heard me.

"Be right there. Get yourself a coffee or something else to drink, to keep your mind busy. I will come as fast as I can." He hung up.

As I replaced the receiver, my mind started replaying all of my plans for Calvin. I guess God had other plans. Hearing the hum of the soda machine in the corner, I followed the pastor's suggestion but didn't see anything I wanted. No, what I wanted was to take Calvin home with me, and watch him be happy and make him laugh. That's all I wanted at the moment.

May 25, 1994

Gem has her diploma. She starts school this fall. My little grandbaby is going to be a college girl. She has many things pulling her in other directions, if she can just finish school, that's all I ask of her. My, but I have been blessed, she wants so much to please me, I may just be successful with her. It's good to see things go well for once.

The farm's a different story. I've had to sell off some of it, but that's just as well, kind of weary of it myself.

Looking to the future,
RM

Chapter Twenty-five

I was surprised by how helpful and caring the hospital staff was being. They contacted the foster mother, Calvin's case worker, even the media. The only hiccup seemed to be where to send his body. For that to happen, I needed release papers from the foster mother. That meant that someone would need to take them to her house. If I went over there myself, I might consider burning the place to the ground. To say I had anger issues toward them would be putting it mildly.

Pastor McClendon came into the family lounge. There was a large bandage on his nose. He was carrying his Bible, and had a trench coat draped over his arm. His hat was wet, dripping water on the floor as he removed it. "You've had a rough night, Kid," he stated as he sat down. Putting his coat and hat on a chair, he opened his Bible and began to read the Beatitudes quietly.

I listened to the familiar words like I had never heard them before. Meek, peacemakers, merciful—all those words were great descriptions of Calvin, and the way he was toward others.

"Calvin said that the angels were here just before his seizure. It was incredible, but I believe it. I don't think Calvin knew how to lie, or even what a lie was. He saw things just as they were."

"You know, Gem," Pastor McClendon said sadly, "what the Devil meant for evil, God can use for good. You might not be able to see it now, but eventually, by His grace and mercy, you will understand."

"Oh, I see it, all right," I said, somewhat angrily. "Evil was done to Calvin over and over. He never did anything but good. There's not a kinder soul on this earth that I know of, and certainly no one as forgiving or appreciative as he is...was." I put my hands to my face. "Oh!" I cried. "I wanted so much for him. I could have given him such a good life. Why, why wouldn't God give me that chance? I don't understand." I balled my hands into fists. "They need to hang that monster that hurt him. No, dying is too good for him." I slammed my fists on the chair's arms.

"You must remember, Gem. How would Calvin treat this man? Even though he hurt him, to death, would he be angry at him?" He leaned in and looked me in the eye.

I was losing some of my fire. "No, he wouldn't. He would be afraid of him, but he wouldn't hurt him back." That I was sure of, because of the way Calvin had walked in a big circle around that creep on the porch at the foster mother's house.

"This terrorist is a lost man." He faced the floor as if he were thinking out loud. "It will just get worse. There will be more of this kind of thing happening. If we are not living in the end times, we sure are close."

"What happened to your face?" I asked, motioning to his bandaged nose.

"Oh," he laughed, putting his hand over the injury. "I had a bit of a fender bender yesterday. That is why I didn't get here sooner."

"What happened?" I asked.

"Well, you know there was this car chase," he chuckled softly. "I just happened to get tangled up in it."

"What?! No, give me details. How did it happen?"

"When the police were chasing the suspect, just after he left your work place, I happened to be going the other direction on the interstate. I had been visiting someone in a hospital here in Knoxville, and was on my way back home." He put his Bible down to have both hands free to gesture. "As they were traveling south, I was going north; this guy comes across the median and *pow*! He smacks right into my front bumper."

"Oh!" I sucked in my breath.

"This," he said pointing to his nose, "is what an airbag that saves your life will do to your nose. The guy flew on by me and came to rest on the shoulder of the highway, pointed in the opposite direction of his original destination." He shrugged. "It was a miracle that no one else was hurt. All this stuff was slung out of the back. It was a real mess. The highway was shut down for hours."

"Wait, was the van a white one?" I jumped to my feet.

"Yes. I guess I helped the cops out, huh? I watched the arrest; it was pretty exciting. If I could never do that again, it'd be too soon." We sat silently for a moment, both hoping never to experience that kind of thing again.

"Here," he patted the chair. "Let's get back to you." He examined my face. "You shouldn't be alone. Come home with me. If you don't, my Mrs. will have my hide."

"You know, a few weeks ago I would have done just that. But now, I think I would like to be alone to think about Calvin, and have time to mourn what could have been." I patted his arm.

"Has our talk helped at all?" he asked.

"Yes, it has helped me to remember what Calvin was like and how he would want me to react. It is a time for meekness and gentleness."

"You know," he wagged a finger at me, "it takes a lot of strength to be meek. Christ had the power to destroy his enemies with just a word, but He saw past their sin and had mercy on them. That is the best example I can think of." He smiled. "I am glad you brought Calvin to church. He was the best listener I think I have ever had. He seemed to hang onto my every word." He laughed. "And his love of the music, it was a wonderful thing to watch. He had such joy."

"You should put that in his eulogy." I said.

"Oh yes, that and much more." He assured me.

As he left, he made me promise to not let myself fall back into depression. I felt a little embarrassed at the memory of that time. I promised him to try to not let that happen again.

Still, I wanted to do something for Calvin. His life being cut so short, I want it to stand for something lasting, and his memory to be more than just a tragedy of terror.

June 2, 1998

So proud of my Gem. She is a college graduate. Her grades
weren't the best, she had some distractions the last term.
She is to be married the end of this month. Not too fond
of her choice. Bobby Jones is clearly the selfish type. I hope
he will treat her right. You've always been good to watch
over her, Lord. No need to back off now. She's going to need
you more than ever. Seems there's going to be a man in our
family after all.

Give me strength,

Ruby Mae

Chapter Twenty-six

Always ready to come to my rescue, George took the release papers to the foster home.

After returning to the hospital, he reported that the lady of the house was steamed about losing her monthly check. Immediately, she was on the phone to get a replacement foster child. It was agreed that she should be denied, and an investigation be launched by the agency.

Upon hearing what the foster mother was planning, I phoned Calvin's new caseworker. Gloria Swan assured me that she would oversee a close inspection of the situation. That was all well and good, but it felt like too little too late. I felt bitter toward the system; It had failed Calvin. I had failed him, too.

When arrangements had been made for Calvin's body to be transported, Carolyn and George, along with the two guards, gave me a ride home. We were all lost in thought. My mind was running over the scene on that Monday morning. I'm glad the terrorist creep didn't get away with what he had planned. But I did wish that he had finished his stealing before Calvin and Mr. Walker entered the greenhouse.

I was dreading the return to an empty house. Having Calvin there had made it more like home again. As we neared the house, I could see that an empty house was far from all of my worries. My driveway was full of media vans. Reporters swarmed the car as George slowly pulled up to the front of the house. The guards helped George get out first, and came around to the passenger side for Carolyn and me. We huddled under their wing spans as questions were fired at us and microphones were shoved in our faces. We managed to squeeze through to the front door and get it open just enough to slide inside, sideways. One guard remained with us, just inside the door, as the other did a sweep through the house.

George's first action was to pull out his cell phone and call law enforcement to have all the media removed from my property. The house was cold and dark inside. Carolyn proceeded to turn on lights and straighten the room.

I could finally breathe a sigh of relief when the last of the media crowd had packed up and gone away. Only the two guards remained, one at the front entrance and one at the rear.

"I guess I should find him something to be buried in," I flatly stated. Carolyn nodded and patted my arm.

As I made my way through the rooms, memories of Calvin flooded my mind. I had images of us sitting together at the table in the kitchen, watching movies on the sofa. The upstairs bathroom brought back a memory of him laughing at his image in the mirror after his shower. When he'd toweled his hair dry, he had rubbed it so hard that it stood up like little springs.

Everywhere I turned, there seemed to be a memory of him. How did that happen so quickly? It had only been a few months since I had met him and yet, it was as if I had always known him.

Ending up in Calvin's room, I picked out his favorite set of clothes for his burial outfit. He had called the new khakis and baby blue polo shirt his church clothes. I gave the room one last look. The dreams I had for Calvin were still there. I could see him sitting at the desk, playing computer games, or lying in the bed, gazing out the bay window. Reaching down, I removed his night light from the wall socket. It was in the shape of a teddy bear. It would normally have been a little juvenile for someone his age, but it was the one he had wanted. The little bear was smiling sweetly.

A noise came from downstairs. That would be Carolyn, still straightening up the living room or preparing a meal. The church ladies had been busy delivering food during the day. Everyone was being so helpful. I suppose it's healing for them.

I started slowly down the stairs, carrying Calvin's clothes. What I saw at the bottom made my heart stop. It was a strange woman, looking up at me. She was heavy set with a bobbed haircut. Her hair was dull and flat like it hadn't been washed for some time. I noticed bruising around her right eye and on her thick arms. Seeing me, she stopped too, straightening herself as if she was ready to do battle.

"May I help you?" I asked, looking around the room for George or Carolyn.

"The lady let me in." She motioned toward the kitchen. "I lied. I told her I was someone from the church."

I could hear noises from the kitchen: plates rattling, and sounds of food preparation.

"Do I know you?" I asked. She did look familiar. I studied her face. This seemed to make her terribly uncomfortable. She looked down, avoiding my eyes.

"I need to know," she paused, rubbing her plump hands together, "are you seeing my husband?"

"Ha!" I laughed. "I'm not seeing anyone. Who is your husband? Just who are you?" I was starting to get irritated. I didn't have time for this monkey business.

"You don't know me?" Her pencil-thin eyebrows went up. "It's me, Becky, Becky Jones. I married Bobby after you kicked him out." She folded her arms defensively across her ample chest.

"What?" The shock hit me hard. I collapsed on the stairs, laughing uncontrollably.

Carolyn and George came into the room.

"What in the Sam Hill is going on in here?" demanded Carolyn.

I managed to point at Becky and spurt out, "Becky here thinks I am having a wild fling with her husband, Bobby Jones. Ha! Isn't that just *grand?*"

Carolyn turned toward Becky, who at this point was beginning to look a little bewildered. "You can't be serious." she stated flatly.

"Oh," I interrupted, "she also thinks that *I* kicked *him* out. How do you like that?" My fit of hysteria was beginning to lose steam.

Carolyn put her hand on her hips. "I don't know what you think, but I will give you the truth. Your *husband* is a woman beater, a coward, and an all-around ass. He beat Gem nearly to death! He killed her baby. And then, he abandoned her for the likes of you. What in the world gave you any idea that she would ever have anything to do with him again?" She stomped her food for emphasis.

"He was saying stuff," she stammered. I was beginning to feel sorry for her. It would seem that we had a lot in common concerning Mr. Bobby Jones. Her bruises told me so.

"Carolyn, look," I pointed. "He's beating her." Laying Calvin's things on the landing, I stood and wrapped my arms around this unfortunate woman. She resisted at first but then slowly relaxed and leaned into me.

Becky began to cry. Her words spilled out in a rush. "Bobby is obsessed with you and your grandmother. It's always Gem this and Ruby Mae that. There's something in this house that he wants. When he's drunk, he says things like, 'I'm going to just go over there and get it.' When I ask what, he smacks me and curses me." She pulled away. "I figured the something he wanted was you." She shrugged. "I mean, look at me. I'm an elephant. Having all those kids and all that stress, I look nothing like I did in my cheerleading days. I look like I ate a cheerleader." She softly laughed at her own remark.

Looking at George, I said, "It all makes sense now."

Turning back to Becky, I said, "I think I know what Bobby wants, and it's not me!"

Opening Grandma Ruby Mae's bottom desk drawer, I pulled out the ledgers.

"My grandmother was a wise woman. She knew that Bobby was poison, and she must have kept him away with a bribe. Here, in this accounting book are all the entries, proof of either blackmail or a payment, depending on how you want to look at it. Either way, it's sure to be illegal."

Turning in the ledger to the pages that contained the entries, I held them up for Becky to see. "Maybe if I tear them out and you give them to Bobby, he will stay away from me and drop this obsession."

"Excuse me, Gem," George interrupted, "may I have a word with you?"

"Sure. Excuse us a moment," I nodded to Becky. George and I stepped into the kitchen.

"Let me scan those pages for you first. Without them, you have no proof of the illegal activity. Or leverage." He smiled sweetly at me. He was right. What was I thinking?

"Yes, please, and thank you George for having a clear head. Will you be able to do that on my old computer?"

He nodded his answer. "Distract Becky for a few minutes."

I returned from the kitchen carrying a tall glass of iced tea and a heaping bowl of peach cobbler.

"Have some refreshments, Becky, while George gets those pages ready for you." I gave a Carolyn a look that said, go along with me on this.

"Yes, Becky," Carolyn said, sugar dripping from her words, "please, do sit and relax while you have a little something and calm yourself."

Becky looked leery, but agreed when she got a good look at the church ladies' succulent dessert.

After a few bites, she commented on how good it was and how nice we all seemed. She then began to talk about her children, how active and smart they were. I could tell by the way her face lit up that her babies were her whole world.

George returned to the room with an envelope. "I hope you realize how seriously we take your husband's criminal activities," he said solemnly. "He could be sued by Miss Wilson for the money that was to be her inheritance. The law tends to frown on extortion. Those amounts were entered with no explanation. Therefore, it's left as an open question of the cause. Given the end result of his relationship with Gem, it doesn't appear beneficial to him for this information to be revealed to law enforcement." George gently handed the envelope to Becky.

She nodded, big eyed, placing her unfinished dessert on the coffee table. She received the envelope from his strong hands. Lowering her gaze, she said, "I think I owe you an apology, Gem."

"Does he hit your children too?" I asked.

"He yells at them, but no, he doesn't hit them. I'm in charge of the discipline. He's gone a lot, so, no, he hasn't hit them—yet." She shook her head hard, the dirty hair not moving.

"The way you say yet tells me that you think he will," remarked Carolyn.

"Get help, Becky," I insisted. "Did you know that my grandmother was instrumental in starting the Women's Crisis Center?"

"Was it because of what happened to you?" she asked.

"No, it was long before that. Ironic though, huh?" I smiled at her.

As she stood to leave, she said, "Thank you all for being so kind. I'm not used to someone being so nice to me. I will give what you told me some serious thought."

I saw her to the door. After closing it, I leaned against it. Carolyn and George looked at me sympathetically. We all just shook our heads.

I hoped Becky would have the courage to get help, and that things were finally finished for me on the issue of Bobby. I hoped to never see him again. An unsettling feeling in my gut told me it was probably wishful thinking.

July 4, 1998

My grandbaby is having a baby. They had the wedding,
minus the shot gun. She hasn't announced it yet, but I can
see all the signs. History seems to repeat itself. I'm not so sure
that the marriage was the best decision. I'm trying to like
her husband. But Lordy, he makes it hard. Never was such
a foolish fellow. He tries me at every turn.

Give me patience, Lord.
RM

Chapter Twenty-seven

After Carolyn and George left, I went to the funeral home with my body-guards in tow, to make arrangements for Calvin's funeral. They would prepare his body and have him taken to the church for the service.

I picked a middle of the line casket, a bronze color that had the soft baby blue lining. It seemed suitable. The bronze seemed masculine, and the light blue color was a soft contrast. I couldn't help touching the pillow where his head would lay. "I'm so sorry," was all I could think to say.

In doing his obituary, I had them put down that upon his death, he was taken away by the angels. He was an orphan to this world, but not to his next one. He would be sadly missed by all of the staff at In the Garden, where he was employed while he was also a student at Clinton High School. I added a special thank you to the doctors and nurses at the hospital for their kindness and mercy. I ended it with the basic information for what time the services would be held at the church with the burial to follow, Reverend McClendon presiding.

Next, I phoned the pastor to confirm the information.

Giving the funeral director a down payment for the services, and Calvin's pressed burial clothes, I concluded my business with them.

Making the arrangements had drained me completely. I sat in my car, thinking about the payments I would be making for the next three years to cover the funeral. I thought about Jeremy Garrett, wondering what he might be doing right now. Mr. Walker came to mind next. I also had an odd feeling about my mother being out there, somewhere. Then the Bobby Jones scene with Becky entered into my thoughts.

I eventually realized I needed to get moving. *Just keep moving, Gem. It will all work out,* "If I just keep moving forward. Right, Heavenly Father?" I prayed.

Returning to the house, I stored Ladybug in the barn, locked the front door behind my protectors after they made a satisfactory sweep through the house, and made my way to my beautiful bedroom. It was still light outside, but I was too weary to want to do anything but prepare for bed.

As I passed by my nightstand, the stack of unread letters caught my eye. My grandmother was still with me, somehow. I kicked off my shoes and snatched the letters up as if they were a lifeline.

Sitting in the window seat, I read the dates to be sure to keep them in sequence. The glue had held for many years, but became brittle as I tore the first of them open.

> Dear Henry,
> I hope this letter finds you well. I have some news that I must share. It is not pleasant, and I hesitate to tell you, given your current circumstances, but it must be said. I am with child. As I am sure you have counted it out, it is impossible for it to be your child. I have been unfaithful. I shall live the rest of my life with the knowledge of my sin. If you can find it in your heart to forgive my weakness, I will live the rest of my life trying to make amends. The doctors tell me that the child will be born in the spring. I hope to be reunited with you and that we will be able to continue as a family.
> Please forgive me; I have never stopped loving you. I have been so very alone and turned to someone else for comfort. It was wrong. I am truly, truly, sorry.
> Ruby Mae

I dropped the letter in disbelief. If Grandpa Henry wasn't my mother's father, then who was? I started the next letter. It was basically the same wording, with the exception of her saying she was concerned that his silence meant he couldn't forgive her. The last letter urged him to respond no matter what he felt. She needed to know that he could forgive her. I remembered the date on his tombstone; it was before the letters were written. He never knew.

None of them revealed who the father, my real grandfather, was. *Man, grandma really knew how to keep a secret.* Everyone thought she was such a saint. I guess even saints are sinners sometimes.

Understanding how loneliness can eat you up, I forgave her. How many did Jesus say? "Seventy times seven." *Let's see; that would be what, four hundred and ninety? I could never do numbers in my head.*

I put the opened letters with the others, in what I had come to call her memory box. My mother's birth certificate was among the paperwork. It had Henry Wilson written in the father's name category. I couldn't think of another person who might even come close to knowing such a delicate piece of information. The only possibility would be the person she had turned to for comfort, as she had put it.

With my nerves ragged, I prepared for bed.

To say I tossed and turned all night would be putting it mildly. It was as if every noise was amplified, every shadow was longer and darker. Even the 360 thread count Egyptian cotton sheets Carolyn had given me felt like barbed wire. Every time I closed my eyes, I was plagued with the image of my grandmother and some mysterious lover. Sometimes his face would be blank; other times it would be a young, virile Cary Grant type character.

My image in the bathroom mirror the next morning confirmed the kind of night I'd had. *I'll need to wear shades today to hide my red eyes and dark circles.* This was not the way I wanted to say goodbye to sweet Calvin. He deserved my full attention today. Although I wouldn't really be saying goodbye; it was more like I would be saying I'll see you later.

Staring at my bleary image, I promised him that I would push all these things aside. He would get a proper goodbye. I would rather have given him a sweet sixteen party. *Do they call it sweet sixteen when the birthday person is a boy? There I go, my mind wandering off again.*

The phone rang, and I was glad for the interruption. *I shouldn't be alone today. I might just go crazy with so many things going around in my head.*

Carolyn's cheery voice was like a cool spring breeze. She and George would be picking me up for the services. I was very much relieved. *Wouldn't it be great if Carolyn took a real liking to the church?* One could hope.

For the service, the organist played "Just a Closer Walk with Thee," tears pouring down her face. Calvin looked so handsome and peaceful. He was wearing a polka dot tie, navy blue with white dots. It was one the pastor had worn that Calvin had admired. That was so very thoughtful of him. The flowers were all white, blues, and purples. This had to be Miss Polly's doing. She knew Calvin's favorites. The church was full, with the exception of the first pew, reserved for family. Carolyn, George, Miss Polly, Mr. Flowers, Mr. Walker, and I sat together on the front pew. Jeremy Garrett came in and sat next to me. I heard some murmuring behind me. I tried to not become distracted; I wanted my focus to be on Calvin. Still, it was good to have this strong man at my side.

Pastor McClendon did a wonderful job with the eulogy. He asked if anyone wanted to say a few words. Surprisingly, person after person stood and gave a testament as to how Calvin had touched their lives. Some were classmates from school. Others were customers of the nursery. It amazed me that given Calvin's limitations, he was able to make such an impact in his young life. There wasn't a dry eye in the place by the time of the closing prayer.

We all moved out to the cemetery, located on the hill above the church. Calvin's coffin was carried by Mr. Flowers, Mr. Walker, and several of the students from his high school. I had chosen the spot next to my baby boy for Calvin; the little lamb on his tombstone still looked like new. I had chosen one with an angel engraving for Calvin. It would be placed a couple of weeks after the burial. *I wish I could have given him my name.* The name Doe seemed like an odd thing to put on the stone. It was as if he was never claimed, stuck in the lost and found box forever.

After all the songs were sung and all the prayers said, everyone began to descend the hill, going back to their lives.

I noticed Officer Garrett having a close conversation with Carolyn and George. She then came over and kissed me on the cheek. "I love you," was all she said. Then she and George began to make their way down the hill. Jeremy Garrett remained behind.

I thanked the Pastor for the excellent job he did with the service, and the thoughtfulness of letting Calvin wear his tie. I should have been a wreck, but I felt surprisingly calm.

We needed to leave so that the workers could get busy with filling the grave with the mound of dirt. They always waited until mourners left to finish their job. After they covered the filled grave with the flower arrangements, it would be finished. I seemed to be having a hard time walking away. Jeremy put his arm around my shoulders and said, "Whenever you're ready, we can go. There's no rush."

"I guess I'm ready as I ever will be," I replied, looking into those green eyes. "See you later, Calvin. I love you." With that we turned, slowly picking our way among the markers for graves that held so many familiar people. I hesitated at Grandma Ruby Mae's. "I love you too, Grandma. I forgive you." It was the least I could do, giving her something she had so desperately wanted and probably had never gotten during her lifetime.

"We have some business to take care of. Do you think you will be ready for it tomorrow?" Jeremy asked.

"The police still want to talk to me? They have their guy. What more do they need?" I was trying not to sound whiny, but it came out that way.

"They want to do a line up," he stated. "This guy has a lot of money behind him, and it's not the police. The feds and Homeland Security are on this one."

"I'll go, if you will take me. How does that sound?" I asked.

"I would be honored," he replied with a slight smile. "I'll call you in the morning."

Carolyn and George were waiting for me on the front steps of the church. They were deep in conversation with Pastor McClendon. The security team stood like statues behind them.

"Be careful," I teased Carolyn, "the Pastor will have you here every time the doors are open."

They all nodded and smiled.

Shaking hands with the Pastor, we said our goodbyes.

It was hard to leave Calvin there. I wanted to run up the hill and tell everyone there had been a mistake, grab him by the hand, and take him home with me.

November 27, 1998

Something's wrong with Gem. She isn't happy in her
marriage. I can tell. She hardly spoke a word all through
Thanksgiving. That husband of hers ate like an animal
and then made some excuse to leave her at the house for the
night. she didn't fight him on it. I'm going to get to the bottom of this She's not herself.

I'm thinking our girls in trouble, Lord.
RM

Chapter Twenty-eight

A fictitious press release had announced that all witnesses had been taken to a private location. Therefore, the media began to lose interest, leaving the front of my property. My bodyguards were also dismissed. I wondered what power had been behind it all, but was grateful to regain my privacy. After everything quieted down at the house, I was finally alone. I decided to go back to the cemetery, to take just one more look.

As I turned into the church parking area, I spotted Mr. Walker's truck. I pulled Ladybug in beside it. The church was quiet and still. All the doors were closed and locked.

I began my climb up the hill to the cemetery. As I approached Calvin's grave, I saw Mr. Walker arranging the flowers on top of the bare earth mound. "He was the best of us," he said, sadly.

"Yes, he was," I agreed, and joined him in his work.

When we were satisfied with the flower placements, we both stood, stretching our backs. "Tell me about my grandmother when she was young," I said, surprised at myself.

"Well," he said, removing his hat and wiping the sweat from his brow with a handkerchief from his back pocket, "That was a long time ago. Why you so interested now?" He didn't sound irritated, just hurt.

"I need some answers, and I think you might be able to help me," I said, looking down the hill. It was less intimidating than looking directly at him.

"She was my girl, but your Grandpa Henry won her over. I don't much like talking about it." He put his hat back on and started down the hill.

"Henry Wilson is not my grandpa," I said really fast.

That stopped him in his tracks. He turned slowly, staring at me wide-eyed.

"How do you know that?" he demanded.

"Grandma wrote him. He had already died, though, so the letter was unopened. In it, she had confessed that she was going to have a child and it wasn't his. He never knew. She must have kept it a secret from the real father, too. I want to know if I still have family out there, other than my elusive mother." I was starting to shake with emotion.

"I'll be damned," he swore. "That Ruby Mae! She told me Henry had come in on leave. If that don't beat all!" He bent backward and made the strangest sounds toward the heavens, wild whooping noises.

"Then you—I mean—you— Are you saying what I think you are saying?" I talked so fast, I was spitting.

"She came to me; she was so alone. Don't fault her for it. One thing led to another. We had always had feelings for each other. We couldn't help ourselves. It was just that one time. How could she keep something so big to herself? After he died, looks like she would have told me." A thought came to him and he stopped.

"What was it you said? How did you know?" he asked.

"I have several of her unopened letters to him. In them, she confessed about being unfaithful and vowed to live the rest of her life trying to make up for the sin she had committed."

"Sooo," he said slowly. "Brenda being my daughter, would make you my granddaughter." He raised his eyebrows as if asking if I would I mind that.

"I guess I could do worse," I teased him. "What a day! I had to say good-bye to Calvin, and I gain a grandfather. Boy, God does work in mysterious ways. Ways, I'm trying to understand."

"Well, Granddaughter, what have you heard from that mother of yours?" he asked in a friendly tone.

"What mother? She is practically non-existent. I haven't laid eyes on her since I was a kid. She did call the hospital the other day, but I didn't know what to say to her." I really didn't want to talk about her. He must have sensed it. He began to speak very softly.

"Yeah, she didn't come around much. I guess her and Ruby Mae didn't get on too well. She was what you could call a real hippie. Always on the move, what with living like a gypsy and all. You were better off with your grandma." He patted my shoulder.

"Well, Grandpa," I said, trying it on. "What do we do now?"

"Maybe we should go have some ice cream and catch up." He offered his crooked arm to assist me down the hill.

There weren't any good ice cream parlors in town anymore, so we settled for a Frosty from Wendy's. As we sat in the truck, he told me stories of meeting my grandmother down by the creek bed, of how they would wade in the water and tell each other their dreams.

"She wanted to run for public office," he said. "She didn't so much want to be a politician, but she felt women could change things for the better just as well as men."

"I could see that," I nodded. "She would have killed them with kindness and had all their money before they knew what hit them."

"Yes, sir, she could talk a cat out of his tail." He laughed.

When we returned to my waiting car, he pulled up beside it and left the engine running. "I'm glad, Gem. I hope you are too," he said timidly. "I know I can be cantankerous sometimes."

"I am glad," I said. Leaning across the seat, I kissed his wrinkled cheek.

He touched the spot and said. "She used to do that, every time we parted."

"Hey, we both have family now! That's a good thing, huh?"

"It sure is! Goodnight, Gem. I guess I'll see you at work Monday. Hey, it just came to me; Polly is your cousin. How about that? Wait till she hears," he said excitedly.

"I have a cousin, and it's Polly," I said, amazed by another revelation.

We both waved as we turned separate directions down the country lane.

At that moment, I realized I wasn't sure where he lived. *I should really pay more attention to things. You never know when it might be important.*

Arriving back home, I took Calvin's night light out of the desk drawer where I had stored it and put it in the wall outlet in my bathroom. It seemed fitting.

I didn't want to think about tomorrow, but the dread of seeing the criminal responsible for killing Calvin was looming over me. *I wonder what they will do to him. There is no punishment that could be bad or hard enough. There will never really be justice.* I hoped they wouldn't diminish Calvin's worth because of his disabilities. All the people who spoke at the funeral service could attest to the difference his life had made to them. *I would like to shoot this guy myself.* I understood why some people would want to retaliate. *Someone who would do what he had planned to do doesn't deserve any chances, of any kind.*

After a checkup phone call from Carolyn, I sat on the sofa thinking over the day. I began to drift off into a dream.

Jeremy Garrett, Calvin, Mr. Walker, Grandma Ruby Mae, and I were having a picnic by the creek. She was teaching Calvin how to play name that plant, a game she had played with me. Then Mr. Walker and Jeremy were teaching him how to fish and arguing over what bait to use.

It was the nicest dream I have ever had.

February 14, 1999

Lord, you know I have no friend like you, but I have murder in my heart. That no account Bobby Jones is a disgrace to humanity. My darling Gem has lost her baby boy. He was so beautiful. I reckon you have our wee one now. Please still my hand, I want revenge! Some people are no earthly good. You avenge us Lord! Heal my sweet Gem, her heart is broken.

Mine too.
RM

Chapter Twenty-nine

A t 8 a.m., the phone rang. I jerked up from the sofa. My neck was in such a cramp that I couldn't straighten my head.

"Hello," I said yawning.

It was Jeremy Garrett. "Good morning," he said cheerfully. He had probably had a great night's sleep, a morning run, a healthy breakfast, and was raring to take on the day. This was all in my head, of course.

"Will you be ready for me to pick you up in about an hour?"

"Sure," I said. I was lying. "Yes... Well, I'll try." I began to feel panic.

"It's okay, there's no rush," he said, sensing my nerves.

"Oh, good," I said, relieved, "because I just woke up. I didn't even get to bed last night. I crashed on the couch."

"Well, at least you won't have to make your bed this morning," he joked.

"You're one of those guys who sees the glass as half full. I like that," I replied.

"I'll see you around nine."

"See you then." I dropped the phone on the sofa, then went to stand in the closet and stare at my clothes. *What does one wear to pick out a murderer from a line up with a really cute and genuinely nice police officer?*

I grabbed a short-sleeved baby blue blouse in honor of Calvin, beige slacks, and my penny loafers.

Glancing at the tub, I decided to take on the multiple shower jets Carolyn had installed for what she claimed to be "the most refreshing shower ever."

Not only was the shower refreshing, it was really fast. I was out and drying my hair in record time.

I grabbed a banana for a quick breakfast and gulped down half a glass of milk with it. I could get some coffee later.

I had just completed combing out my hair and brushing my teeth when up pulled Jeremy in his patrol car. I had never been in a patrol car before. I wondered if he would be insulted if I asked him to take Ladybug. As he stepped out in full uniform, I realized what a bad idea that would be.

"Did you have any trouble finding the house?" I asked as he climbed the steps to the porch.

"Oh, no, I knew where you lived." He blushed and looked down. "I mean, I have been by here before."

"Okay then, I'll just grab my purse and lock up." *Why am I so nervous? This is just a guy. There is nothing to be nervous about.*

He held the door for me as I sat in his patrol car. I was glad I didn't have to sit in the back behind the metal grill separating the front and back seats. There were so many buttons and lights on the dash, I was afraid to touch anything. He pushed a computer screen out of my way and said, "Seat belt, please."

"Oh, of course, I always wear one. I was just so distracted by all the bells and whistles, and buttons and switches. I'm an idiot, pay no attention to me." I put my hands over my eyes.

"It's okay. I know you have had a few rough days, maybe even years?" He cocked a golden eyebrow at me. Then he smiled. "I will be beside you all the way. You have nothing to fear and no reason to be nervous."

He thought picking out the terrorist was what was making me nervous. If he only knew what being this close to him was doing to my insides and how my palms were sweating.

"Want to run the siren?" he laughed.

"No! You will scare all my neighbors to death."

With a chuckle, he pulled out.

"Where are we going exactly?" I asked, realizing I hadn't even wondered.

"Well, it will be quite a drive. They closed Brushy Mountain, so the nearest federal institution is toward Cookeville. It looks like we will be spending the whole day together. I guess I should have told you beforehand. It just never seemed like a good time," he said apologetically.

"Officer Garrett, it would be terrific to spend a day with you." I beamed at him.

He grinned back. It was such a wide grin that I for once understood the ear to ear description I had only read about in books.

We traveled for almost two hours before stopping for coffee in Crossville. I told him all about my meeting with Mr. Walker the evening before, and our discovery. He was pleased and surprised, knowing my grandmother's spotless reputation.

He told me all about growing up in Clinton and playing football for the Clinton Dragons. He had an older sister who now lived and worked as an administrative assistant to a medical company in Knoxville. She had two sons, and was divorced. His father had passed away from a heart attack several years ago, but his mother was still very active and living a full life. He laughed about her joining the Red Hat Ladies Society Club. He was afraid he might get a call someday, saying she had been arrested for spying or espionage. She sounded like quite a character.

"So," I asked timidly, "did you ever marry?"

"Sue and I were married for five years. I am not sure if being a cop's wife was too much for her, or if I wasn't enough for her. She was repeatedly unfaithful. A guy who I'd thought was a good buddy of mine was one of her interests. That did it for me. There's not enough counseling in the world to scrub that out of your mind." He shrugged.

"Sounds like you tried to make it work. That's more than most people do these days." I studied his face. "I'm sorry that happened to you," I said.

"Same here, about what happened to you. We survivors need to stick together, huh?" He winked. Looking at his watch, he said, "We should get going."

We remained quiet, both lost in thought for some time. The squawking and beeping of his radio and the soft swoosh of traffic were the only sounds.

As we neared the prison complex, Jeremy reached over and squeezed my hand.

"Right by your side, he promised.

I nodded to let him know I was okay.

He answered questions concerning our presence at the guard station. We then traveled through several gates. There was barbed wire on top of all the fencing, and the buildings were the blinding color of bright, white granite.

As Jeremy pulled into another guarded lot, two men in black suits met us at our parking space. "Follow me, Miss Wilson," said the taller of the two.

Jeremy leaped to my side. They didn't say anything to him. I was thinking that all this was prearranged.

When we entered the building, we were welcomed with a cool blast of air. The two suits guided us into a side office. "They will brief you in here," said the shorter man.

A kindly-looking older gentleman was seated behind a computer. I gathered he wasn't too pleased with us. He looked put out, but in a patient way. "We need to move fast. I would have rather have had you here early than late."

"How late are we?" I asked.

"Never mind," he said, looking at his watch. "It was just hard to wrangle enough Arab-looking guys into one place at one time to keep everybody happy. It isn't your problem. Have a seat, Miss Wilson."

It made me uneasy that everyone seemed to know my name. I took the plastic seat next to his desk, and Jeremy stood behind me. The two suits leaned against the wall next to the door.

"I want you to go in there, examine each one closely, and try to be one hundred percent sure of which man committed the alleged crime. When you have spotted him, simply point him out and we will have him step forward, turn to one side, turn to the other side, and then step back. If you are not sure, we will give you more time and have the others do the same movements. Do you understand?" He clasped his hands together on top of his desk.

"Yes, I understand. Would it be possible for me to speak to him? There are a lot of things I would like to say to him" I said, determined.

They all began to shake their heads. "No way," he waved his hands in the air. The two suits moved away from the wall and folded their arms.

I can't say why I wanted to speak to this animal. At that moment, I felt like it was my chance to finally stand up for myself and Calvin. I had chickened out when it came to facing Bobby when he was being so cruel to me. I hadn't demanded more information about my heritage from my mother or my grandmother. When my mother called the hospital room, I didn't give her the tongue lashing she deserved. When that creep at the foster home was mean to Calvin, I did nothing. And here I was again, facing someone that has taken something precious from my life. I wanted a showdown.

"What's the problem with that?" I asked. "You have him in custody. He can't hurt me now. And another thing; why am I even here? Didn't you catch him red-handed?" I was becoming angry. It seemed like the criminal had all the rights.

Jeremy reached down and touched me on my right shoulder, the one with the crick in it of course. He was giving me comfort, more than he even realized. It had a calming effect on me, but it didn't make me want to back down.

"All my life, I have followed the rules, tried to do the right thing. And here this monster is; he doesn't care about rules, just destroying and killing. I want to tell him who he killed, how special Calvin was. I want him to know that it doesn't have to be this way. We can all live together. That was what Calvin was about. He didn't see color, or religion. He saw a possible friend in everyone." I crossed my arms, mimicking the two suits.

"It's not him that you need to fear, Miss Wilson. If he sees your face again, and recalls you, you could be in danger. It could happen when you are grocery shopping, or on your way to work one morning. Someone who is still out there could and probably would harm you. Now, to answer your question about why we need you to identify him, the downside to trying to keep this guy in here is that he had connections, connections with big money. An eyewitness will ensure that he cannot walk." He sat back in his seat and put his clasped hands behind his head.

"What about Mr. Walker?" Jeremy asked.

"He was hit from behind, and didn't get a good enough look at him. Miss Wilson had a face-to-face look. She even struck the guy in the nose. You'll be glad to know that it is still bruised." He smiled.

The two suits shuffled their feet. I don't think they were too happy with the older man for mentioning the suspect had a bruised nose.

"Easy, Charlie, don't compromise the case," said the taller one.

"Will it be all right if Gem writes her feelings down in a letter?" asked Jeremy.

The three men looked at each other and nodded in unison. "Yeah," said the desk guy. "That will work. How about it, Miss Wilson?"

I shrugged. "I guess it will have to do. May I have a pen and some paper?"

After they supplied me with writing materials, I began a manifesto that would have made the Pope in Rome proud. I explained simple common human decency and the right of every human to exist, no matter their race, gender, religion, or mental capacity. I gave a description of Calvin's gentle and loving demeanor, and how he had touched so many lives. I ended the letter with a plea to stop this madness of destruction, and for the people of these terrorist groups to find and hold to the original beliefs of the Muslim religion: beliefs of peace and harmony, not of death and ruin.

The older man looked the letter over. He then said, "He will probably wipe his butt with it, but at least you got to say what you needed to without putting yourself in danger."

I felt his comment was uncalled for, but he was probably right. The kind of people who destroy others for rivers of honey and 72 virgins aren't playing with a full deck.

We went into the darkened room. The only light was from the staging area where six men were standing in a row. A height scale was painted on the wall behind their heads. I began studying the bearded faces from left to right. The second one from the end was the guy. *I would know his ugly mug anywhere.* There was some bruising on his nose. I was glad I had hurt him. It felt good to fight back. *I think I will take it up.*

"Second from the right," I told the men in the suits.

They did the routine, having him step forward and turn both ways.

"Yes, that is him," I confirmed, pleased that he would pay.

After I had signed their documents on the dotted line, we were released. I was so very relieved to get out of that place and have it behind me.

May 21, 1999

Gem is finally free of that monster husband of hers.
Hallelujah! She still won't press charges, just mopes
around when she's home. Not sure how she's doing at
work. I don't think she likes her job anymore. I hear
her crying at night. Heal her Lord. Another thing,
please set my stomach straight. It's been hurting something awful. I'd be so grateful.

Ruby Mae

Chapter Thirty

On the way back to Clinton, Jeremy and I stopped for some dinner at a Shoney's. Everyone turned to stare at the policeman coming into the restaurant as the waitress led us to our table.

"Do you ever feel uncomfortable with all the looks?" I asked.

"Sometimes, but not as much as when I first started," he said.

"I have enjoyed the day, even though it has been a really strange one." I said as we slid into a booth.

The waitress interrupted our conversation. "How are we today? Are you ready to order?" she asked, holding her pad high in the air.

"You first, please," said Jeremy.

"May I have a club sandwich and a glass of milk?" I requested.

"All right, Miss. And you Sir, what can I get you?" She turned toward Jeremy.

"I'll have the same, thank you." He handed her our menus.

"You are such a gentleman."

"That's something I learned from my parents. Manners were top priority in our home. It was considered to be insulting to others if you didn't show respect. It has served me well, and I plan on teaching it to my children if I am ever blessed with them." He grinned.

"I think you would make an excellent father." I grinned back.

With the rest of the meal, our conversation was light and easy. We joked about the suited, serious men at the prison and about my new relative discoveries.

On the last leg of our trip, Jeremy turned his scanner down. He was off duty, with the exception of delivering me home. The warm, setting sun was coming through the back windows at a sharp angle, casting a long shadow in front of us. I never wanted to stop. I wanted to just keep going like this forever.

But, like all good things, it ended. In this case, with us turning into my driveway. It looked more like a parking lot. Evan Walker's truck, Carolyn's BMW, Mr. Flower's and Miss Polly's work truck, Mr. and Mrs. Johnson's Crown Victoria, and Pastor McClendon's Honda were all crowding the edges of the gravel driveway.

"Looks like a party," remarked Jeremy.

He cut the engine and I turned to him. "While we are still alone, I want you to know how much I appreciate your taking me today. I couldn't have done it on my own. You were wonderful, and I hope that... Well, not to be too forward, I hope we can spend more time together."

Before I could blink, he put his arm on the back of the seat and leaned in to kiss me.

It was soft, sweet, warm, and it was gentle.

After the kiss, he stayed close to my face. "Oh, Gem, you are truly that: a Gem. I want to know everything about you. I want to spend a much time as possible with you, if you'll have me. We will take it slow if you want, or at the speed of light. I don't care which. I just want to be around you. I feel so right with you. I am myself, only better. What do you say? Will you take a chance on me?"

My eyes began to water. I choked out, "Yes, Jeremy. Oh, yes."

With that he kissed me again. It wasn't as gentle, this time; it was passionate, but it was still just as sweet.

Giggling like a couple of teenagers, we staggered out of the car and up the steps.

Before we reached the door, Carolyn jerked it open. "Hey, what's going on here?" She eyed us up and down with curiosity.

"Later." I winked at her. She gave me that knowing look. She knew, by the blush in my cheeks that Officer Jeremiah Garrett and I were becoming a couple.

All of the others greeted us as we came in the door. Evan, AKA Grandpa Walker, gave me a bear hug. Miss Polly practically picked me up off the floor. "Hey, Cuz!" she exclaimed. Pastor McClendon pumped my hand and searched my face as if he had some questions and might find the answers there.

Mr. and Mrs. Johnson just nodded a greeting. "We are glad to see you are doing fine, Child," said Mr. Johnson, as Mrs. Johnson tearfully held her hanky to her nose.

"Well, I am glad you are all here," I said. "Is this a special occasion, or has something else happened that I should know about?"

"It's more like a family reunion," boomed Jack Flowers as he came out of the kitchen with George, carrying a tray of lemonade and glasses. "Let's all have our refreshment on the veranda." Jack sat the refreshment tray on the dining room table and passed everyone a glass.

"That's a great idea," said Miss Polly.

"Before we go out," George said, "Carolyn and I have an announcement." He looked over at her, and she came to his side. With their arms around each other, they looked into each other's eyes. "By the first of the year," George began, but couldn't finish; he was choking up.

"We will be having a baby," squealed Carolyn.

"Oh, how wonderful! A baby!" I wrapped my arms around them both.

There were hugs and handshakes all around. Everyone was so pleased.

My company stayed late into the night. We ate the wonderful leftovers that the church ladies' Bereavement Committee had provided, and told story after story about each other. By the end of the evening, many new relationships had been formed.

Jeremy was the last to leave. He stole one more kiss from me before making a date—the old standby, dinner and a movie—for the next Friday night.

By this point, my head was spinning. As I was straightening up things in the kitchen, the phone rang. I assumed it was Jeremy, or Carolyn wanting to talk about Jeremy, but there was a surprise caller on the other end.

"Hey, miss me already?" I answered.

"Gemini?" It was my mother.

I recognized her voice; it had a business-like ring. "Sorry, I thought you were someone else."

"I am sorry to call so late," she apologized.

Yeah, about fifteen years late, I was thinking. I didn't respond to her apology.

She continued, "With all that has happened in the news lately, I would like to reconnect with you, if you think that's cool." I didn't respond.

"Anyway, the deal is, I have some important rallies coming up in October and I would like to have your input. It could make a big difference. The subject is one with which you have just had a great deal of experience. It involves enlightening the public and the powers that be on the impact of terrorism for our country. I would appreciate it if you could speak at the rally. It's in D.C." She paused.

"You don't know me." I started. Closing my eyes, I pictured myself earlier that day with Jeremy beside me, and the courage I had felt in writing the letter at the prison.

"I won't be speaking at any rally. You have never been, and most likely will never be, a mother to me. I have had it with you finding so many more causes around the world to fight for, and your neglect toward me. I cannot continue this question of whether or not you are going to be in my life. It is obvious to me now what that answer is. You are the most self-centered, unloving person I have the misfortune to have been a product of. Before I slam the receiver into your ear, have the decency to answer some questions that have haunted me my entire life. Why? Why did you dump me at Grandma's? Why didn't you come back for me? What happened to me at the commune?" I held my breath.

"I don't look back," she said flatly. "I only look forward. I was no good for you. My mother needed someone to care for, and I couldn't give you the care you needed. The commune was a bad place for a little girl. There were men there who were doing things to you, things I couldn't stop. So, I did what I thought was the best solution. It is something I live with every day. That is why I am trying to make a difference in this world. There are things out there that I *can* change. What happened with you, I cannot change. I know you had a good life, a better one than I could have given you." Her voice was stern and stilted.

"Still, I can't call you mother, and I don't know who my father is." I waited.

"Neither do I", she responded. "There were so many. You have heard about the father complex. I looked for love in every man who would pay any attention to me, and lots of them did. It was that way in the commune. They called it free love. Free it wasn't, love, it wasn't either. It was a nightmare that still haunts me. Maybe I am running still, but I can make a difference out here. And I would like your help. It's something we can do together. It could bring healing between us, maybe, on some level."

I was becoming confused. I was losing the hold on my anger. I could see her point. It is hard to be the grown up sometimes. I swallowed my pride. It went down hard.

"Maybe, so," I responded. "We could try. But I am not a speech writer."

"Just your story, in your own words, that is all you need to say. I am sure you will do great." She sounded much relieved.

"Your father lives," I said. "He is actually Evan Walker. Maybe you could work on your father issues with him. As for you and me, it will take some time. I am not so trusting anymore. When I was a little girl, Grandma always said 'don't judge, lest you be judged.' That's from the Bible, and I try to live that. I want to live that."

"Sounds like good advice," she responded. "Evan Walker, huh? Wasn't he an old beau of Mother's?" she asked.

"Yes, he was. You should contact him. He asked about you just yesterday, after he discovered that he was your father."

"Maybe I will." She spoke slowly, making me wonder if she would.

We ended our conversation with a promise to be in contact. I wasn't so sure it would happen, but the part of me that is weak wanted to give her the benefit of a doubt.

September 4, 1999

Everyone's excited about the Labor Day Festival at the County Fair. This is the first year that I won't have an entry. It seems my blue ribbon days are over. Gem can't pull out of her blues enough to be interested. She's quit her job to care for me, I've got the big C. Such a loving girl she is, as soon as I told her, she set her jaw and announced how we were going to beat this. But, it's a losing battle. I'll not see another year.

Give her strength to get through this, Lord. I'm puzzled at your ways right now.

RM

Chapter Thirty-one

So many things have happened in the last two years, so many good things. Looking back, it is hard to believe that I was so unhappy just a few short years ago.

One of the best things to happen is that I am a godmother to Alexis Carol Woodward. She was born to proud dad George and mom Carolyn on Valentine's Day, very fitting, considering what a sweetheart she is. When Carolyn has an out of town assignment, I am her delighted caregiver. She calls me Mamma Em. The G sound still eludes her, even at the age of two.

Jeremy and I have set a date for our wedding. We will be married in a few days, on Christmas Eve. To say we have taken it slow would be an understatement. But once you have been burned, it is wise to take it slowly. This will be forever for us both. And we are enjoying the ride.

Carolyn is pulling out all the stops to plan our wedding, and we are delighted that Alexis will be old enough to be our little flower girl. Grandpa Evan has been practicing giving me away. Jeremy has asked George to be his best man, and a fellow officer friend, Ben, to be a groomsman. Carolyn, of course will be my maid of honor, along with Jeremy's sister as a bridesmaid.

In the Garden will be providing the flowers, with a reception to follow at George and Carolyn's spacious, radically decorated home.

After the wedding, Jeremy and I will be traveling to the Smoky Mountains for our honeymoon, where we will hike, picnic, ski, and get to know each other in the most magical, intimate way. I am thrilled, and terrified at the same time. Don't even think about the 'just like riding the bike' theory. I really don't think that is a fair comparison; there are no handle bars to hold on to for steering, or brakes to stop with when it comes to love. If you fall while riding a bike, knees and elbows get scrapped or bones get broken. When it comes to love, your heart is at risk.

When I change my name to Mrs. Garrett, I am thinking of changing my other names as well. I will no longer be known as Gemini Rainbow Wilson, but as Gem Mae Garrett, in honor of my grandmother. But there will still be rainbows in my life.

I continue to miss Calvin at work, every day. I don't know when or if that will ever end. Jack Flowers erected a monument in our Little Eden, dedicating the garden spot to his memory. Other special needs children from the high school are working there now. We have a girl named Callie, who is petrified of touching dirt. We have special gloves for her to wear. This school year also brought us a boy named Sam with cerebral palsy, who has a fetish for water. He gets mesmerized, watching it run out of the hose. Grandpa Evan has taken him under his wing. The two are inseparable. Anytime Sam is there, he is by his side. Callie has Down Syndrome, but is very high functioning. She is everybody's friend. I often find her in the office, talking Cousin Polly's ear off—a feat not easily done.

As for the relationship with my mother, I went to DC and made a somewhat unsuccessful speech. It was strange to be around her again. She was businesslike, cool and distant. At the end of the poorly-attended rally, we both agreed that I was not made for public speaking. She hasn't asked me back again, and I don't expect to hear from her much. I do hope she will come to the wedding, but I am not hanging onto it. She has stayed in contact with Grandpa Evan. She calls him from time to time to report on what adventure she is on. He then reports back to me. But the calls are coming farther apart, and we both know that they will end entirely someday. It's okay; we have that understanding and are fine with it. I think it comes under the heading of not missing what you don't have.

Pastor McClendon has worked wonders with Carolyn. She, George, Jeremy, and I sit together in Bible study and church services most Sundays. When I asked her why the change of heart, she just shrugged and said that it was time to let go of some bad things and grab on to some good ones. I didn't press her. If she ever wants to confide in me as to why she had a church phobia, I will be there for her.

As for Becky and Bobby Jones, we heard through the grapevine via Mrs. Johnson, that they were divorced not long after she visited me. With the help of the Women's Shelter, she regained her freedom, her figure, and had begun attending college. Poor old Bobby was back living with his mother, and developing an even bigger drinking problem. Mrs. Johnson reported that Becky's edge over Bobby was some kind of blackmail. Apparently, she had used the ledger book copies as leverage to gain her independence and keep Bobby at bay. See, cheerleaders are smart. I for one am very happy for her and her children.

If Bobby Jones has crossed my path again, I am not aware of it. Having a big strapping policeman for a fiancé can be a real deterrent for those who mean you any kind of harm.

We are all still waiting for the terrorist, whose name I still cannot pronounce, to come to trial. Our President had all the detainees, as they are calling them now, moved to another location. The rate of justice movement isn't quite just. I feel for the families who have lost loved ones to these people, and for the ones that have sacrificed their lives to make the changes to keep our world safe. I can see where right is becoming wrong, and it is very confusing and unsettling. It all makes no sense. So, what do you do when something makes no sense whatsoever? You just pray that it all turns out all right and do what you can, when you can.

I am trying to not become too excited about the wedding. I have a fear of jinxing myself if I get too comfortable. Carolyn has asked me to not worry, to leave it all in her capable hands. Jeremy has no concerns about the ceremony; he is more interested in the marriage. Why do I still have this nagging little voice saying, "watch out" in the back of my head?

January 1, 2000

We're all still here. Apparently, the myths of computers crashing and wide spread mayhem were a bunch of hooey. We are heading into the 21 century just fine, thank you. Although, I won't be seeing much of it. Hate to think of what I'll miss. The house is looking spiffy. Gem has redone every nook and cranny. She should be out having fun with friends instead of nursing a hopeless cause like me. Don't know where she'll go when all is said and done.

Sorryfully,
Ruby Mae

Chapter Thirty-two

My dress was tea length, made of a soft ivory lace material. My bouquet was made of brilliant red and glowing white roses. I touched them all one more time to be sure that they were real before returning them to the cool of the refrigerator. I could hardly believe I was heading to the church for our wedding rehearsal.

The sanctuary looked like a dream with the afternoon sunlight pouring through the stained-glass windows. A soft glow was cast on the entire room. The smiling faces of Carolyn, George, Pastor Mc-Clendon, friends, and family greeted me.

As we started to practice our movements for the ceremony, the front door of the church burst open. Cold air and a loud voice filled the sanctuary.

"You said 'til death do us part!" boomed a very drunken Bobby Jones. "That means one of us should be dead," he slurred loudly.

So, here it was. The snake had crawled out from under his rock and was rearing his ugly head. My first thought was, *what would Grandma Ruby Mae do?*

Jeremy and George simultaneously moved toward him. Grabbing both of his arms, they proceeded to drag him outside.

I caught up with them and waved them away. "I got this!" I said emphatically. They looked at me like I had lost my mind.

"This guy is crazy drunk, Gem," said Jeremy. "He shouldn't be here. This is a special night for us, and I won't let him ruin it."

"You're right," I nodded in agreement. "But before you have him arrested, I want to give him something that is long overdue."

Bobby was looking a little deflated, like he was in need of some more liquid courage. He had stopped struggling and was staring at the ground.

Jeremy and George reluctantly released him. He staggered a bit before laying his head sideways and looking up at me with an evil leer.

"You have no power over me," I spoke sternly and clearly. "I am not the young, ignorant girl you married. She died when you killed the baby inside her with your bare hands. I am a different woman now, and you will never hurt me again." It felt so good to say those words, because I believed them. I could see from his defeated expression that he believed them too.

When the officer arrived and assisted Bobby into the back seat of the patrol car, he stared straight ahead and didn't say a word. I was hoping he had finally heard me. But, if he did cause me any more trouble, I was ready for him. I could face him now.

We continued on with the rehearsal and had a lovely dinner afterward at Jeremy's mother's home. There was some nervous laughter, but nothing was mentioned about the earlier events of the afternoon. George and Carolyn insisted I spend my last night of being single at their house. I couldn't refuse the pleas of sweet Alexis. She pulled at me with her little hands, "Pease, pease, Mama Em?" Who could say no to that? I was a goner; I would do anything she asked of me.

It was hard to say goodnight to Jeremy. But I could do it confidently, knowing that the next time I saw him, we would never be parted again.

The day has finally arrived. It is Christmas Eve, and by this evening, I will be an old married lady. The morning of our wedding, Grandpa Evan stopped by to escort me to the church. He had a surprise gift for me. He presented me with a gold necklace, accented with a single stone: a ruby that was my grandmother's when they were courting. The jewel had originally been the setting of her engagement ring from him. Even though she had returned the ring to him, it was a precious reminder of the love they shared. I was speechless, and so grateful to him for such a thoughtful and loving gift.

Walking down that aisle toward Jeremy standing at the end, my hand cupping Grandpa Evan's arm, was like walking toward a dream of belonging somewhere: a future full of hope, a beginning for making new and happy memories.

It was a great day. I could feel Calvin and Ruby Mae there with me, being so happy for me. The only thing that could have made it perfect would be, if they could have been there in person.

When Pastor McClendon announced, "You may kiss your bride," Jeremy said, "I would love nothing more, but first I have something to say to her." He turned to me, and holding both my hands, he looked into my eyes. "Today, we start a new life. We have both had disappointments and loss. Together, we can face anything. Together we are stronger. The love and compassion you had for your grandmother Ruby Mae and Calvin tells me everything I ever needed to know about what kind of wife and mother you will be. I am so blessed to share in that love." With tears in his eyes, he gave me our wedding kiss.

The elaborate reception Carolyn had planned was a blur to me. I was swimming in the look of adoration in my husband's eyes.

I like the outcome of my life. I just wish I had known that I could do it all and come out all right. The best thing is that I am surrounded by people that care for me. I have more family and friends now than I know what to do with. I have hope in this beautiful relationship with Jeremy, and the possibility of a family of our own.

I still have my Ladybug and our home. It is good to know that some things last, and the other things you need could come along at any given time. The day in and day out of living can be such struggle. But just like a rainbow spanning across the sky, like most lives, it can become a thing of beauty, created from a storm.

April 4, 2000

I have a feeling that this could be my last
entry, Lord. I'll see you soon and Gem's little boy,
and my Henry. I hope he's not too upset with how
things went between us. Watch over my Gem. Give
her a good life and the chance to love and be
loved. I pray that my Brenda will come back to
you and her souls not lost forever. Be extra good
to my beloved. You know who he is. I'm ready to
fly home, anytime you say.

RM

About the Author

Rita Rumgay grew up just south of the Cumberland Gap in Claiborne County and in Knoxville in East Tennessee. Her childhood was split between living with grandparents on a farm eight miles outside New Tazewell on top of a ridge and in the city of Knoxville with her Mother and two siblings.

She has worked in a factory, the library system, and business offices for the University of Tennessee, a legal firm, and a Baptist church.

She received an Associates Degree from Pellissippi State Community College in Office Systems Technology with a concentration in Business and is a member of Phi Theta Kappa Honor Society and Blue Star Mothers.

She now resides in Knoxville with her Husband Ken, four sons, one with special needs, and a delightful granddaughter. Shared by them all, are their loving pets, Elsa the dog and Stella the cat.

Coming Soon

Have you ever wanted a "do-over," a second chance at restarting your life? Do you ask yourself, how did I end up here? Just like frustrated teenagers, sometimes moms want to run away from home. What would happen if the expectant husband and ungrateful kids had to do the laundry, wash the dishes, cook all the meals, and find their own constantly lost, things?

This mom is ready to bust out, leave her dead end job, escape the cluttered, frustrating home, and find laughter, excitement, peace, and herself, whoever that is now.

All she needs is a plan. It's time to push the re-set button on her life.

www.ingramcontent.com/pod-product-compliance
Lightning Source LLC
Chambersburg PA
CBHW070750180626
46818CB00007B/3063